"PERHAPS HE'S ASLEEP."

Basil stepped toward the slumped figure. He touched him gently on the shoulder. Leon slowly moved forward until his head clunked on the desk.

"I'd say he's been dead for a day or two. Let's not touch anything," Basil sensibly warned just as Sara was about to pick up the phone.

"There's no blood," Hortense reflected, peering around Leon's body. "Poison? Strangulation? Fright?"

"Dear, you're favoring the insidious. People do die quite often on their own steam."

Hortense dismissed the dull fact even before she noticed the thin multicolored cable beside the body.

"Aha, strangled by a computer cable."

————————— ★ —————————

"This is entertainment!"
—*Library Journal*

ALL BOOKED UP

TERRIE CURRAN

WORLDWIDE®

TORONTO · NEW YORK · LONDON · PARIS
AMSTERDAM · STOCKHOLM · HAMBURG
ATHENS · MILAN · TOKYO · SYDNEY

ALL BOOKED UP

A Worldwide Mystery/July 1989

First published by Dodd, Mead & Company, Inc.

ISBN 0-373-26028-8

For the guys

ONE

"I'M TERRIBLY SORRY, SIR," Ms. Gluck announced sanctimoniously, peering above her reading glasses. "The volume, as numbered, is not on our shelves." The manner in which Edwina Gluck handed the request slip back to the slightly portly gentleman with the scattered white hair hinted at satisfaction. Had she charge of library policy, the reins on circulation would certainly be tightened.

Basil Killingsley, not accustomed to being in error, nor to being treated as a feckless browser, received the slip with openmouthed astonishment. He drew in his chin, tilted his head, and bulged his small, pale eyes at Ms. Gluck. His good breeding struggled against the moment's inclination and narrowly triumphed as he suppressed a haughty "preposterous!" He swallowed, easing down the gall of indignation, and cleared his throat.

"Are you certain? 1527/-H5? Perhaps you misread my five? Higden's *Polychronicon*? Wynkyn de Worde's fourteen ninety-five edition?"

Ms. Gluck crackled with professional patience and pretended to look at the slip.

"Yes. I *can* read," she said with more edge than she intended. "No, I did not misread the call number or the title. As to the edition, I'm sorry, but we do not own a fourteen ninety-five Wynkyn de Worde *Polychronicon*—"

"Oh, but you *do*!" Basil insisted spiritedly, as if in fact Ms. Gluck had the item in question on her person and for some perverse reason refused to give it over.

Ms. Gluck was touchy about being challenged on bibliographic matters, especially absent volumes, as she had been called on the carpet more than once in recent times over just such matters. However, as she was not one to air library laundry in front of a stranger, she pressed her offense by widening her beady brown eyes and sitting stiffly upright.

"I beg your pardon?"

"I said you most certainly do! Own a fourteen ninety-five *Polychronicon* printed by Wynkyn de Worde, that is. First English text with musical notation," he added, as if the distinguishing feature would trigger some recollection in the stubborn librarian's mind.

Professor Basil Killingsley held his ground so tenaciously that Ms. Gluck was forced, for a moment, to consider the possibility of her own error. Ridiculous. Perhaps Cyril Prout, she thought, casting about for a victim. Might he be getting a bit dusty in the brain pan? No. Cyril Prout, the curator of rare books, was quite on top of things, and certainly of things within his professional purview. Ms. Gluck pulled herself up straight as if to offer height as evidence of authority.

"We—that is, the Smedley, does not own that particular volume. We do have a modest collection of Higden in later editions—"

"I don't give a hoot about later editions. Good Lord, he's even in paperback: excerpted from a fourteen eighty edition by Caxton and going in the vicinity of seven dollars. Penguin, I believe. But I'm not the least concerned with Higden or his foolish history of Britain. I'm concerned with that particular edition—"

"Which, I repeat, we do not own." Ms. Gluck's staccato syllables were calculated to pummel her adversary's eardrums and thereby put an end to the silly exchange. Basil, summoning patience garnered over thirty-five years of teaching medieval English history to college students who didn't know one Henry from another, was not about to let this shred of obstinate ignorance escape.

"Madam, it was not a month ago—" (he calculated weeks back through June and May on his fingertips) "—five weeks at the outside—that I handled the very volume I have here numbered, 1527/-H5, right in these hallowed halls. I took it into the reading room over there," (he indicated the direction to his right rear with a rise of his frizzy white brows,) "and I carefully perused the imprint and each of the signatures." Basil's happy recollection mollified his pique. "Quite a fine specimen: excellent condition, all signatures complete, colophon, endsheets, original binding covers, too, as I recall. Quite rare. Worth a goodly sum, I'd say—"

"No doubt, if, however, we were fortunate enough to own such a rarity," Ms. Gluck entuned with a touch of insolence.

"Not a question of *if*, Madam—"

"Gluck. *Ms.* Gluck."

"How do you do, Ms. Gluck. Basil Killingsley here. Professor or doctor, as you wish."

Ah, one of those, Edwina Gluck thought, her gaze riding down her narrow nose dispassionately. "Perhaps, Professor Killingsby—"

"*Ley*. Killings*ley*."

"Ah. Killings*ley*. Perhaps you'd care to check the card catalog? Though if Dr. Prout, our rare books curator, says it's not ours, I'm afraid it's not ours." Her cold, thin smile was not calculated to persuade.

"I don't need to check the catalog, Ms. Gluck. I know the call number by heart—"

"Of *course* you do, Basil," Hortense Killingsley merrily caroled to cap her husband's ineluctable stubbornness, as she entered the archway to the circulation desk. She was fanning her face with a magazine and puffing dramatically. She trundled closer, stooped to give her husband a peck on his pink cheek, and sized up the situation. "Basil knows a great deal by heart," she confided to the librarian, cheerfully clutching her large flowered purse in a tight hammerlock and waving her magazine in Ms. Gluck's direction, "and I must say he is rarely mistaken in his claims." She resumed her fanning.

Ms. Gluck eyed the mangled purse and then the damp face of the large arrival across the marble counter. Her close-set eyes narrowed as if they had sighted something vaguely offensive. Hortense, reassessing the level of discourse to be several notches below good humor, quickly added, "Rarely, of course, is *not* always, is it, Basil? And the car's air-conditioning is out again. I suspect we could do better pouring Freon in our ears."

Basil peered blandly at his wife and closed his eyes to summon control. He would ignore the mechanical, not the human, failures his wife raised.

"Quite so. Rarely is *not* always. However, in *this* case," he challenged the librarian, "I am definitely not mistaken."

"And what case is this, dear?" Hortense asked, checking her watch.

Ms. Gluck rolled her birdy eyes upward to the domed ceiling, sniffed, adjusted her glasses, and hastened an escape to another inquirer several feet away with whom her sphere of effectiveness might be greater.

Before Basil could enter into an appropriate tenor of explanation, his wife begged him to be swift as the groceries were melting in the car and they had agreed that she'd pick him up at three and here it was fifteen after. Basil went straight to the point by offering up his request slip as proof of his argument.

"Dear, why not do as that woman suggests and check the catalog? Now, now, I've no doubt that you've got the right number, but you might have the wrong library."

The thought struck Basil as patently absurd. However, before releasing the full brunt of his indignity on his ubiquitously sensible wife, he attempted dispassionate reconsideration. In the four or five weeks since the end of the academic year, he and Hortense had made exploratory visits to several research libraries in the Boston area in order to line up their summer fun. He had researched and examined many fine incunabula that tickled his English historian's fancy.

"It might be at that charming little mausoleum—the John—no, Annmary Brown Memorial—"

"Yes, dear. Charming. No," he asserted with absolute certainty, "Ranulf Higden—the fourteen ninety-five Ranulf Higden—is not with Annmary Brown. There's a copy at the Hay Library, but it's in shabby condition. Positively shabby—even shows signs of being doctored. Wretched job." Hortense tsked in complete sympathy. "The mint Higden is—or *was* in the very recent past—right here in the Smedley, and right here in my hands."

"Then all we need do is to check the catalog and show the entry to that dour woman who will then apologize profusely for casting aspersions on your infallible—nearly infallible—memory."

Basil sighed. History demonstrated his wife's direction to be right in more than one case. He shrugged his shoulders and bowed in mock obeisance. The couple nodded to each other and headed for the catalog room beyond the cool marble lobby, to the relief of Ms. Gluck, who was surreptitiously watching from behind some unlikely fronds.

As Basil shuffled through the H's and the Higden entries and past them to High and on to Hight, he readjusted his glasses and began again.

"Shall I try under Ranulf?" Hortense cautiously queried, "or better, under whatshisname, the printer—"

"Wynkyn de Worde. Yes, try him. It's got to be cross-indexed."

"Wynkyn or Worde? Or de Worde?"

Basil was trying to maintain hold on the remnants of his sangfroid as he reshuffled among the Higdens.

His preoccupation was signal for Hortense to exercise
her own considerable investigatory judgment.

A third run-through produced only further frustra-
tion and sent Basil to the Ranulfs, where he met his
wife parked on a stool. They were now of equal height,
eyeball to eyeball.

"No luck?" she asked, curbing her exasperation.
"I've ransacked the Wynkyns, Wordes, and de
Wordes along with every possible variation, all to no
avail. Actually, they've a fair sampling of the fellow's
printed editions, even his fifteen twenty *Cronicles of
Englonde*—that's the quasi-King Arthur business,
isn't it? But they haven't a single Higden incunabulum."

"Impossible! I can't be getting dotty, can I, dear?"

Hortense drew back and gave him a wide-eyed stare.
She tapped her magazine on her chin.

"I believe dotty has been heretofore reserved for
women of a certain age and disposition. However, far
be it from me to hog the term generically. In any case,
dear, the only indication of your dottiness is your
novel suggestion of it."

His wife's assessment accepted, Basil plowed on:
"No, no, I'm positive Ranulf Higden was here five
weeks ago."

"Perhaps he's on vacation?"

"I'm going to check this out with that Trout—or
Prout fellow—the rare books man. If he's worth his
salt, he's bound to know of it."

"Dear, the groceries..."

"This will take only a moment. Consider it an in-
vestment in my sanity." He patted his wife's warm

pink cheek and rushed off, leaving her to trail after if she chose.

From the cessation of gesticulations and muffled mumblings in the catalog room, Ms. Gluck surmised the imminent return of the weird couple. She braced herself, folded her hands on the speckled countertop, and made a concerted effort to appraise the wall moldings as Basil, not the least bit humbled by his lack of evidence, strode over. Glints of savage tenacity darted from his gooseberry eyes.

"Now look, Ms. Gluck, I've no doubt that you run a tight ship around here, but there's definitely a leak somewhere."

"You didn't find your Higden in the catalog?"

"No, I didn't find my Higden in the catalog, as you say. But it is—was—here and if I have to spend the night searching—"

"Now, now, Professor, we all make mistakes. Why, I myself, just the other day..." she trailed off looking around for a dog to pat.

"Ms. Gluck. I must ask to see the rare books curator, Dr. Prout, is it?"

"I'm afraid Dr. Prout is at a meeting," she announced mendaciously, "and isn't expected back for the rest of the afternoon. I shall, of course, alert him to your problem first thing in the morning." Examination of her stringy fingers occupied the greater share of her concern.

"The missing Higden is not so much *my* problem, Ms. Gluck, as it is the Smedley's—even, one might say, the whole scholarly world's."

Edwina Gluck sniffed, faintly suspicious of the professor's rush to the metaphysical. She looked down

her thin, straight nose at the countertop and reexam-
ined her fingers as if waiting for a diamond to appear. "Perhaps you'd care to see our assistant director,
Dr. Tewksbury? I believe she's . . ." Ms. Gluck looked
about vaguely. "Ah, there she is now."

Dr. Tewksbury caught Ms. Gluck's signal for help
out of the corner of her eye. Her central focus, however, was on the large-framed bustling woman in front
of her strangling a rolled-up magazine and crushing a
flowered fabric purse to a pink alligatored bosom. She
was insisting that something that wasn't there should
be there, or something that was there, wasn't there. In
any case, Sara Tewksbury was forcibly riveted by the
animated manner (if not the matter) of this aging
preppy.

"And Dr. Tewksbury, while Basil has his gaps,
when it comes to Things That Matter, I would stake
my Cuisinart on him."

"And Ranulf Higden's *Polychronicon* matters to
him?" Sara asked, without the slightest suggestion of
irony.

"The fourteen ninety-five Wynkyn de Worde Ranulf Higden *Polychronicon*, yes, that matters to him."

Why that should be so did not cross either woman's mind. Both were of the school that understood
about Things That Matter. No whys or wherefores
clouded their thinking, no peering into existential
voids for them, no struggling to wrench out Meaning
or Purpose. It was simply there or not.

"Ah, there he is now: remonstrating with that Ms.
Gluck. She's certainly short on humor, and heaven
knows how much one needs it with Basil, especially
when he's on one of his hunts."

Hortense gestured for Basil to come over to meet a sensible woman. Ms. Gluck coolly directed Basil's attention to his wife's breathy "yoo-hoos" and cautious waves.

Though Basil eschewed generalizations about members of the human race, librarians were exempt. Ms. Gluck was evidently a librarian. This tall woman with his wife—this woman in yards of gauze and tiger-tooth jewelry—was decidedly not a librarian. Or not an ordinary librarian. By God, she was taller than Hortense by a good two inches, and certainly leaner by a wider margin. As his mind was about to wander in the insistent direction of Sara Tewksbury's sartorial extravagance, his wife made introductions so Basil might swiftly clarify his version of the situation.

Dr. Tewksbury, arms folded over her braless breasts, had already gleaned from Hortense a variety of clues on matters bibliographic and beyond. Now, largely for Basil's benefit, she slouched a bit on one hip, nodded, tsked, and gave every indication of concern.

"And there's no listing in the card catalog and yet you handled the volume yourself?"

"Yes. Four or five weeks ago. It was most assuredly in the catalog then."

"I don't doubt it. I sometimes wonder that thieves don't walk off with the shelves as well." Sara waved a bebangled arm in the air.

The Killingsleys looked at each other as if the brutal fact of theft had never occurred to them, certainly not in connection with library material.

"It's endemic with research libraries," Sara advertised. "I guess we've got snob appeal. Studies show philosophers grab the bulk because they can concoct the best rationalizations for stealing.''

Hortense rushed in to obviate suspicion. "Basil is not a philosopher. Not in the academic sense. He's rational—and speculative, to be sure, though largely about things medieval. Surely that doesn't qualify?''

"My dear, I am certain that Dr. Tewksbury holds me blameless of Smedley thefts.'' Basil jutted his frizzy brows to the odd librarian, just to be sure.

"Hmm" Sara crooned, cryptically pivoting her chin with her hand, "you've got something of the suspicious butler look..."

Basil, sniffing which way the wind was blowing, settled for having the problem, if not himself, taken seriously.

"Suspect as I might be, I cannot persuade myself that it was I who took Ranulf Higden.''

"Okay, then.'' Sara smiled and went on efficiently, pushing back her bracelets. "First, we'll check our computerized listings—though the chances of it turning up there are nil. We're just beginning to shift over to computers and our director has given the open-stack items priority, so rare books and manuscripts won't be systematically entered until God knows when.'' Sara threw up her hands and allowed them to fall back on her loosely draped hips. Her jewelry jangled. Ms. Gluck shot out a disapproving look.

"It'll take forever, but we simply haven't the staff to go at it whole hog. You know,'' she confided to the couple, "librarians are absolute troglodytes about computers. It took *years* to convince some to replace pencil entries with ID card machines, and now computers...!''

Sara's exasperation at her conservative colleagues billowed over every now and then on whomsoever happened to be around. In this case the whomsoevers were entirely sympathetic.

The Killingsleys were very much of the space age in technological innovation. In fact, despite their sixty-odd years and professional interests in the remote historic and linguistic past, both Basil and Hortense were mechanistic freaks. They were already into their second-generation computer (which did all but bind and publish their typescript). They had a VCR, CD, tape decks, stereo TV, satellite dish, electronic slide rules (one never knew, Hortense was fond of saying), food processors, poppers, choppers, juicers and slicers, microwave ovens, and every lesser variety of electronic gadget invented. As further proof of their modernity, they had signed up (and put cash down) to be among the first commercial travelers to the moon, and were negotiating on the preservation of their bodies cryogenically.

"You're not computerized?" Hortense asked incredulously.

"I am," Sara declared, "but the Smedley's not." Her small joke was heeded by only one of the Killingsleys. Basil was too distracted by what he could only label a conundrum. Sara returned to business. "We should check the serial catalog—just on the far-off chance that this Higden is not ours. In any event, we'll locate all known copies and move from there."

Basil nodded, allowing the possibility of his fallibility its tiny inroad.

"Of *course*, Basil," his wife sighed in recognition of a sensible path. "How silly of us not to have thought of that instantly! What with one thing and another and that rather unhelpful Ms. Gluck . . . well, I imagine she sees her share of oddities. And then what with the groceries—oh, goodness, the groceries! It's been—'' Hortense checked her watch and was horrified. ''My word! Maggots will get to the meat, to say nothing of the curdling that is occurring even as we speak—Oh, you must excuse me, Dr. Tewksbury, but I see you've got matters under control. Basil, you will simply have to use your own pedestrian means to get home. I cannot wait a moment more, however eager I am for results. Thank you, Dr. Tewksbury. I feel Basil's in competent hands.'' Hortense extended hers and shook Sara's. Despite the row of outlandish bracelets jangling down the arm, Sara's was a good, solid handshake. Substantial. With a nod to her husband, Hortense turned and strode purposefully down the central staircase.

''Have you checked with Cyril Prout?'' Sara asked, turning back to her charge. ''He's our rare books curator. He's been with us only a few months, but he seems to be right in there.''

Basil nodded thoughtfully. Prudence, however, dictated a prior visit to the serial catalogs in the reference room.

''My wife is, I must admit, frequently correct. Always has a firm eye on the forest. I'm a tree man, myself,'' he said with awkward humor, looking up at the tall woman as if she might sprout leaves.

The two of them divided directions, with Basil going off to the reference room and the serial catalogs and Sara heading for the computer terminal at the far end of the circulation desk. She was more concerned about

the Higden than she let on, though she reminded herself that the odds favored a flawed recollection as opposed to a missing incunabulum. On the other hand,
she was thinking as she typed in the appropriate information and waited for the bleeps, this wouldn't be
the first loss, particularly from rare books. And there
was little or no question of misshelving there. Furthermore, her sagging spirit noted as INFORMATION
DOES NOT COMPUTE. PLEASE TRY AGAIN flashed on the
screen, it's one thing to have a missing volume, but
quite another to be missing the card catalog entry as
well. It's as if the item did not exist—or someone was
careful to make it seem that way.

Just for surety's sake, Sara Tewksbury retyped her
entry, tapped her maroon nails on the plastic monitor
as it electronically digested the information, and then
again flashed up INFORMATION DOES NOT COMPUTE.
PLEASE TRY AGAIN. She repressed taking direct action
of the sort her colleagues would approve—punching
the screen—and was distracted by a commotion across
the marble lobby. The source was, of course, Professor Killingsley, glasses perched atop his upturned nose,
white hairs flaring in the breeze created by his haste.
He was fleeing with a large, open volume in his arms,
followed by a panicky reference librarian who was
giving all indications that nothing short of her long-
preserved virginity was now in doubt, and that Basil—
the fleeing man—was principally responsible.

"Oh...oh..." she crooned mournfully.

Winifred Sisson stood paralyzed at the threshold,
torn between leaving her station and preventing a
shocking felony. Stretching on tiptoe, she squealed,
"You mustn't—you can't," all the while struggling to

uphold the cardinal library rule for silence. "I say, reference material must be used only in the reference room," she breathily repeated, flapping her arms.

Basil kept up his pace, treating as rhetorical the frantic cries of Miss Sisson, for so she wished to be addressed despite Ms. Gluck's singular example.

"I have it!" he whispered with a fair degree of force. "By George, I found it!"

Fortunately, the archway between the lobby and the circulation desk area was triple width, as Basil wasn't paying heed to mundane details of wall placement. All his faculties were focused on a particular spot in the large volume that he wished to bring to the attention of anyone who might possibly share his concern. Both Edwina Gluck and Sara Tewksbury were simultaneously alerted. Each chose her own form of response: Ms. Gluck's was to note pressing business with the potted plants at the extreme end of the circulation desk, and Sara Tewksbury's was to prepare for cardiopulmonary resuscitation on Miss Sisson.

"It's all right, Miss Sisson. I'll take responsibility for the reference book—and for the professor. You may return to your station."

Basil was oblivious to the stir he was causing and nearly crashed into Sara who had placed herself in his path. The sounds of her barbaric jewelry alerted him.

"Ah, you see," he stage-whispered, "here it is!" His finger tapped about three inches from the top of the page.

Sara bent over to focus better on the complex listing, and gently led Basil to place the heavy book on the circulation desktop. His finger did not shift a millimeter.

"'Higden, Ranulf, d. 1364. Policronicon//West-minster. Wynkyn de Worde, 1495. 50 p.l. cccxlvi (i.e. 347) f., 1.1. illus. (music). G. van Os wd R. 26cm (f°.).' That's it, Dr. Tewksbury—the one with musi-cal notations. And here, copies: DCL (naturally), NN (oh, I'd forgotten that), CtY, hmmm. Ah, here, SmD. That's it, the Smedley. Well, what can we say to that?" Basil pronounced smugly.

Sara took charge of the volume, *The National Union Catalog Pre-1956 Imprints*. She shifted the large pages back to the imprint and hooked her abun-dant red wavy hair behind her ears.

"You see, Professor, this catalog was published in 1973."

"Oh, um, I see. Then its contents are valid only up to—and probably something before—nineteen sev-enty-three?"

"Mmm. It means the Smedley—at the least—had the Higden up to seventy-two or seventy-three. It might have been traded or sold anytime after."

"But I tell you it wasn't, or rather, it wasn't up till five weeks ago." Basil was beginning to hear petu-lance in his repeated assertion. He lowered his tem-peramental register.

"Surely if you sold it or whatever in the last five weeks, someone—the Prout fellow—would be aware—"

"Oh, yes. As a matter of fact—" she looked up thoughtfully "—any sale or acquisition of rare mate-rial is something of an event for the Smedley and all administrative staff are in on negotiations. Come to think of it, we haven't sold anything along these lines

in years, not since the oil crunch wrecked our bud-
get.''

"Then I'm right and you do still have—or should
have—the Higden?''

"Right.''

"Oh.''

TWO

THOUGH BASIL KILLINGSLEY felt vindicated, he did not feel satisfied. While the assistant director went off to question Cyril Prout, the rare books curator, Basil cradled volume 245 of *The National Union Catalog* in his arms, hoping to reach a larger audience with his precious cargo.

Striding across the lobby from the opposite direction with his arms full of books was pimply Herman Lobel, aiming for the reading room to dispatch his load. He was absentmindedly humming a tune of no discernible melody and paying no heed to the slightly portly gentleman moving in equal oblivion crosswise toward the reference room, his arms also weighted with a single oversized tome. The two preoccupied persons collided.

"Oops."

"Pardon."

The pimply fellow's several unsecured volumes toppled, and while both grappled to retrieve them, they succeeded in scattering more. Herman rushed to close those that fell open, while Basil, constitutionally incapable of handling anything in print without absorbing some of its contents, glanced at the several titles and call numbers. Herman Lobel was nervously smirking and grabbing books as fast as he could realign them in his arms. Basil stacked a last one on top of the fellow's pile and bent to pick up his own hefty volume. As he did so, Herman, too eager to flee, knocked into the frizzy-haired professor again, scattering a few books once more.

"Don't worry, son," Basil patiently assured the fellow, "I'll just stay down here, pass up your items, and remain stationary while your youthful vigor takes you to your destination."

This Marx Brothers routine was witnessed by several persons, each of whom placed different significance on the scene. Ms. Gluck at circulation stood tall in smug confirmation of her long-standing belief that such and like mishandling occur when laypeople are given free access to library material; a lanky, baggy-trousered fellow, having halted at the reading room entrance (but perceiving no philosophic ground for his involvement) beheld the commotion with distant bemusement; and there was Miss Sisson, the reference room librarian, still paralyzed in panic at the door of her station, chewing her nails in fear that she would be personally charged for damages to volume 245.

Basil Killingsley—to say nothing of Herman Lobel, who scooted into the reading room hunched over his burden—took no notice of the observers, but was distracted from his monomaniacal pursuit of the 1495 Higden. His mind's eye replayed the clumsy happening of moments before. In doing so, that inner eye seemed to read repetitive titles. (Or was he perhaps victim of his wife's dangerous prevalence of imagination?) He saw himself on his knees with the pimply fellow scurrying to close book covers, but not before his inner eye caught several *Songs and Sonnets*. He well knew that there was nothing peculiar in such a title; in fact, the English Renaissance was top-heavy with just such—His flypaper mind riveted on Renaissance, juxtaposed it with *Songs and Sonnets* by...um, Henry Haward—no, Lord Henry Haward late Earl of Surrey...yes, yes, otherwise known as good old Tottel's *Miscellany*.

What sharpened this rather weird line of association into focus was the fact that Basil had not long since found a Tottel amid the Carolingian Renaissance ("such as it was," he always added to indicate its dubious status as renaissance). At first he relegated its placement to ignorance between *the* Renaissance and the overrated Carolingian flurry of interest in things cultural. When he later recalled the misplacement to his wife, she heartily agreed and irrefutably demonstrated the linguistic basis of such absurdity.

"You know how those lacking any sort of classical sense will bandy about naissance and renaissance as if they were synonymous with any spurt of artistic activity. I mean really, Basil, when you stop to think about it, the Western world's experienced (according to some!) upward of a dozen renaissances in the last millennium. One barely has time to fade and pass on before another wave of cultural enthusiasm is thrust upon us as pure Renaissance. Carolingian, Tenth Century, Twelfth, Quattrocento, Elizabethan, Augustan—well, now I ask you, how many were legitimate renaissances?"

Basil had followed his wife for most of the argument and decided in favor of whatever original line of thought he had had in raising the issue of Tottel rather than feeding Hortense's intellectual dudgeon. Nonetheless, Tottel's Elizabethan Renaissance *Miscellany* that Basil stumbled on in Carolingian archives was puzzling more for its call number than for the legitimacy of its company. The call number on its spine was right in line with its Carolingian confreres. To Basil's mind, a part-time underpaid shelver might well be careless about eras, but those who assign call numbers were professionals. He intended to bring the discrepancy to the attention of some Smedley staff person, but the moment's scholarly pursuit took precedence, especially as it had been near closing time.

Basil's find had occurred several weeks earlier, and as with others who had made like finds of (mostly) Tottel in unlikely locations, the matter passed from his mind and the editions remained where they were. Or at least some of them did.

Indeed, Herman's generosity (though not his identity), had not gone unnoticed by some of the more vigilant of the Smedley staff, but who would bother to fuss about a Tottel here or a Tottel there? Besides, any indication of irregularity was apt to redound to the reporter of such.

As Basil's brain was computing the confluence of titles, persons, and eras triggered by his collision with the pudgy, pimply fellow, Sara Tewksbury returned from rare books where she left the curator, Cyril Prout, tearing at his few, sparse hairs.

"Oh, there you are, Professor Killingsley. I'm afraid the Higden business isn't looking good and we ought to inform the director. I'd appreciate it if you and the *Union Catalog* came along since Giles isn't one to cope well with this sort of news."

Indeed, theft was not an activity Giles Moraise chose to acknowledge. No one at the Smedley could honestly say they had ever heard the director utter the syllable; rather, he employed the most optimistic of euphemisms ("misshelved," or "temporarily missing") to deal with ugly reality. Theft, loss, misplacement, whatever—a rare edition was nowhere to be found and Sara knew her boss was apt to deny the fact or blame her lack of vigilance, and might even hint at her complicity.

"He's not violent, is he?"

"No. But he's got high blood pressure and the sight of me alone tends to have an undesirable effect on his condition."

"Well, if you don't think we're rushing to conclusions? Hortense is always saying how I flail first and consider after. That's not true, of course, but—"

"Feel free to flail; Giles won't notice. As a matter of fact, he's in the middle of annual staff evaluations and I'm pretty sure he's working on mine, ransacking his thesaurus to find the perfect pejoratives."

On the way down the hall Sara gave an incredulous Basil a capsule summary of her tenure at the Smedley, beginning almost a decade ago when Giles had appointed himself principal mobilizer of forces to deny her the assistant job.

"He knew I was qualified, but he took offense at my unfeminine height and outlandish attire. I was one of those sixties students, and as director of a distinguished research institution, he was not about to have the Smedley invaded by beats, hippies, yippies, frippies, whatever—no such oddball riffraff in his library. Not, of course, until he lost the litigation and the court ordered the Smedley to hire me at several thousand dollars more than the advertised rate. So here we are."

And there they were at the boss's door, it being instantly opened with uncharacteristic enthusiasm, indeed, with an effusiveness suggesting Sara's arrival as nothing short of salvific. She smelled a rat.

"Ah, come in, Dr. Tewksbury. I was afraid you might be off saving nuns in El Salvador or beached whales on the Cape."

"No, Mr. Moraise. I am quite present and efficiently carrying on my duties. Of course, I always have a petition for some desperate cause on my person."

"Ah, yes, of course," he chuckled unpleasantly. "Please come in and be polite to Mr. Cecil Blinn from Dallas. Mr. Blinn, Dr. Tewksbury, my, uhum, assistant. And—and with whom do I have the pleasure?" he concluded, suspiciously eyeing Basil Killingsley.

"Giles—" Sara began, leaving off her introductions, coming as they did in the midst of his and the rise of Cecil Blinn.

"Ceese to my friends. Howdy, ma'am." He stood up to his full Texan height, and grinned at Sara's companionable stature.

"How do you do—" Sara checked out Giles's face for the appropriate form of address. His slit mouth was silently registering sibilants. "—Ceese," she tentatively spoke, offering her bejeweled hand.

"Mighty fine, ma'am, mighty fine." Ceese shook it with gusto, causing a metallic clamor that rode up Giles's spine. "Nice to see a tall woman. You from Texas?" He chuckled.

Sara smiled in return, glad that there was a cushion of good humor in the otherwise turgid atmosphere her boss generated.

"Oh, as I was saying Giles, Ceese, this is Professor Killingsley and, well, perhaps we've come at a wrong time...?"

A wave of confusion swept over Cecil Blinn's large, round face suggesting dread of being abandoned. He acted quickly.

"Nope, not for me. Your boss here was just giving me an earful about operations."

The boss grinned and nodded officiously from his leather swivel chair.

Sara got the picture. Giles was doing his best to woo a wealthy prospect. Evidently he was just about out of marbles with the Texan, who was trying to exact good value for his donated dollar.

"You bein' second in command, as they say—" Giles's lips compressed slightly at the thought "—well, I guess you should be in on my plans. And your professor friend here, too. Any friend o' yours is a friend o' mine."

Ceese grinned and offered seats to each of them. Giles passed his hand slowly down his face to compose a more rigid visage. After all, it was his office, money or no money.

"Sure's a big book you got there, Professor." Before Basil could assume the limelight and captivate this small audience with his curious news, Ceese bulldozed right on. "And that's what I'm here about. Big books, big bucks." He chuckled as Giles's eyes rolled in motionless sockets and Basil cocked his head in scientific interest. "You folks see, I'm hereabouts to spread some cash in fair trade for some culture!" He smiled broadly as if his logic were complete. Giles Moraise and Basil Killingsley maintained their rigid postures.

"Ah—" Sara jumped in to keep the goodwill flowing "—may I ask where your mon—cash comes from? I'll bet Texas oil."

"Right-o...ma'am." Cecil hesitated, hoping to gain a first-name basis. "I've been real lucky and so's now I got some catching up to do in my ed-yu-cation." He grinned some more, pleased as anyone could be with himself, his cash, and his plan. He continued to elaborate on his pleasing themes. "So's I took myself East to where all the intellect-yu-als are." He smiled expansively as if Giles, Sara, and the professor constituted the bulk of Eastern intelligentsia. "Great-Granddaddy Blinn got himself a year's ed-yu-cation at Harvard, but he took off to the Boer War and never came back. By the time the Blinn line got to my daddy, the wheat farm was nothin' but a dirt farm and there weren't much of a market for dirt. 'Ceptin' what's under it." Ceese winked at Sara knowingly, and she turned to her boss.

Giles Moraise was taking pains, though not great ones, to appear other than his boorish self. He was grinning with unwitting maliciousness from behind his large, leather-tooled desk, interlocking and tapping his pudgy fingers over his bulging vest. He leaned forward and toyed with his expensive fountain pen, searching for a path to move things along.

"Ahem, I would gather, Mr. Blinn—"

"Ceese to my friends."

"Ah, yes, um, Ceese, I would gather that your finances improved dramatically during last decade's oil shortage—"

"Hell, yeah! Boy, did I make out like a reg-yu-lar bandit. Oh, not so much as them A-rab fellas, but I done myself real proud. But don't get me wrong. I ain't no greedy hog. I been givin' lots away to the local schools and every which charity, but I figure it's high time I got me some general highbrow learnin'."

"Have you considered continuing education?" Basil asked, concerned that the generous fellow follow the most expeditious path to wisdom.

"Hell, no. I ain't got much to continue and I can't sit still in a classroom at my age. Not that I'm an old fogy, mind you," he added for Sara's benefit.

"Ah, but Mr.—Ceese—" Basil moved toward the edge of his seat, still clinging to the open *Union Catalog* on his lap. He was so taken by this Rabelaisian thirst for education that he momentarily forgot his purpose and was preparing to dissertate on the innovative opportunities for adult education in modern America. However, Giles Moraise, fearing that Cecil Blinn's generosity would get diverted to some avenue other than the Smedley, cut short Basil's pedagogical review.

"Yes, but Mr.—Ceese is particularly interested in the Smedley, well, shall we say for family reasons...?"

"My wife's—my ex-wife's family—used to talk o' this place as if they owned it, but Giles here was tellin' me he never heard of the Nooklins—"

"I said—"

"No need to go apologizin'. They were always goin' on in hoity-toity fashion claimin' all kinds of things. But I'll tell you—" Ceese leaned earnestly toward Sara "—there weren't a nickel between 'em and so they gets their daughter married off to me. Didn't last but a few years before I see them all spendin' my money—that was okay by me—but not them then turnin' around and makin' like I was dirt..."

The Smedley administrators as well as the academic bystander were uncomfortable with the fellow's recitation of his personal life, though Sara was intrigued by his refreshing sincerity.

"And so you hope to..." she trailed off, pointing the course back to the Smedley and away from Mr. Blinn's familial one-upmanship.

"No, don't go gettin' me wrong. What's done is done and I ain't hopin' to thumb my nose at the Nooklins. Nope, it just struck me that the Smedley here might just be a place to begin, seein' as how I heard so much about it. Nope, what I might do for you folks is between us and I won't be needin' public advertisements." He sat back, contented that his motives were clear and aboveboard.

"Well, yes," Giles smiled, "perhaps you'd like to hear a bit about our operation?" Without checking for a response, Giles cast about for an appropriate beginning only to have his eye catch sight of Basil Killingsley innocently sitting along the left wall in the tufted goose-wing chair. A portion of Giles's brain strained to recall what the slightly portly stranger was doing there with the large tome on his lap. Nonetheless, the financial resources ("big bucks") Cecil Blinn represented refocused the greedy director's thoughts.

He had to impress the Texan with Eastern eminence—his own as well as the Smedley's. To this end, he led Ceese, whose admitted acquaintance with libraries was slim, down ridiculously sophisticated paths.

"... and we've got a modest showing of medievaliana, some incunabula internationally recognized—"

"That's them early-day books?"

"Yes. Pre-fifteen o one, also known as—"

"Wow hee! Bet there ain't a mess of 'em around!"

"Ahem. Actually, in relative terms, of course, there are quite a few. What makes one item more valuable than another is condition and edition. Certainly the text is a major determinant; after all—" Giles Moraise looked down at his twiddling fingers and warned himself not to appear too patronizing "—a Caxton Chaucer's value is infinitely higher than that of the Chronicles of Bartholamaeus or a *Philobiblion*, regardless—"

"I beg to differ." Basil stirred from his preoccupation with the *Union Catalog* Higden entry, pushed his glasses up his nose bridge, and leaned forward. "The Bartholamaeus work—do you have it?"

Giles squinted in Basil's direction but said nothing.

"Oh, I don't mean to dispute your generalization, Mr. Moraise. No, not at all. Indeed, a Caxton Chaucer is worth more on the market. However, at the risk of sounding pedantic, I think it prudent to indicate that the Bartholamaeus suffers from prejudice incurred—rightfully, I might add—from the rather pedestrian company it is forced to join. Some quite dreadful. Mark my words—" Basil raised the index

finger of his right hand, reserving his left to hold
Higden to the page ""—the day will come—""

"Yes, yes, of course, um, Professor." Giles grabbed
the floor by sheer force of volume and continued,
specifically directing himself to Cecil Blinn. "As I was
saying, it's not just a question of literary worth, but
one of quantity. I believe the professor here will agree
that there are very few Chaucers and quite a few
chronicles, sermons, and, of course, tomes of bad
verse." He smiled and pulled in his pudding face, his
best shot at congeniality.

"Right-o. Always comes down to numbers. So how
much is that there Chaucer worth?"

"Well, a good first edition Caxton—fourteen eighty
or thereabouts—unfortunately their extreme scarcity,
to say nothing of considerations of condition
and completeness, makes them just about unobtain-
able—"

"Ah," Basil burst in, unable to let a half-truth slip
by, "I beg to differ—"

Ceese was amazed to see such controversy generated from an avenue of discourse he never dreamed
existed. He turned eagerly to Basil. "How much,
Professor, huh?"

Giles fought back a scowl and the bile rising in his
esophagus.

"Really, Mr.—Ceese—I'm quite sure there isn't one
for sale anywhere in the world today, despite the professor's groundless objections."

"I beg your pardon, but—"

"Professor Whatever-your-name-is, I stake my
reputation on the fact that there isn't a single first
edition Caxton Chaucer available at this moment."

"A fourteen eighty Caxton Chaucer?"

"Yes, a fourteen eighty Caxton Chaucer," Giles mimicked. "Nowhere."

"I am not expert as to the availability of Caxton Chaucers—" Basil feigned concession and saw Giles melt with feigned relief "—however, I do know that Caxton's first edition of Chaucer... We *are* speaking of *The Canterbury Tales* and not some lesser, albeit first-rate, work?" Giles nodded generously, gothically bridging his fingertips. "In which case the first edition is fourteen seventy-eight and not fourteen eighty." Basil nodded once to cap his point and receded to the straight back of the tufted chair.

Cecil Blinn's porcine eyes bulged and moved from Basil to Giles where they rested, waiting for the gauntlet to be flung back.

Giles rubbed his eyes and squeezed the bridge of his nose.

"Fourteen eighty or *thereabouts* I believe might be liberally interpreted to include fourteen seventy-eight. In any case," Giles rushed on with clear tonal indication that he did not wish to pursue the deplorably petty issue, "there isn't one for sale on this planet at this moment."

"Not for a million bucks?" Ceese asked in astonishment. In his world, even allowing for inflation, a million bucks could at least get conversation going.

Sara thought it time to separate the approaching clash of values before Giles exploded with some subcultural obscenity causing who knew how much to march out the door.

"Well, you know, Ceese, market value isn't easy to assess. I guess something like the Caxton Chaucer is in league with a Rembrandt—"

"This here Chaucer book is somethin' to look at?"

"No, actually not," Sara had to admit, foreseeing the next explanatory pitfall. "Caxton—the printer—wasn't much on aesth—on the visual side of things. His importance lies in selecting texts that then dictated literary posterity." Oh, God, she thought, I'm sounding like Giles.

"So what you're saying is that it ain't much to look at and you can't hardly read it and it's worth more than a body will sell it for. Wowee! That sure is looney!" Cecil Blinn's large pink face was aglow with amazement.

Sara watched Giles's plastered smile crack at the corners. "Giles has told you of some of our needs?"

"Why, no, ma'am, we were just gettin' to that."

"Yes. I was just about to outline various options for Ceese—depending, naturally, on the size and conditions of his generosity."

"You should know that the Smedley's in desperate need of an improved security system and complete computerization of our special holdings," Sara announced.

Giles Moraise bolted upright in his chair, cleared his throat, and searched his desktop for some direction to obfuscate the one raised by his idiot assistant.

"Are you sayin' that stuff is gettin' heisted around here?"

Basil's torso darted forward, nearly letting slip the large volume on his lap. Theft, that obscene act, had again been raised in connection with the very life-blood of the scholarly world.

"No, no, no, no." Giles hastily guffawed, hoping to obscure any hint of scandal. "What Dr. Tewksbury means is that we've got to keep up with the times. Yes, keep up with the times. And we do. Why, even as we speak..." Giles rolled his eyeballs up to his twelve-foot ceiling to avoid Sara's vaguely contemptuous look, but caught the professor's frenzied rise from his chair with the heavy tome.

"Even as we speak, my good fellow—" Basil picked up Giles's ball and ran to his own hoop "—someone (I hesitate to be alarmist and say 'they') has indeed been—dare I use this gentleman's term and say 'heisted'? an exceedingly rare edition of Ranulf Higden's *Polychronicon*, fourteen ninety-five Wynkyn de Worde printing." Basil came round to Giles's desk side and placed volume 245 of *The National Union Catalog* squarely in front of him, tapping the Higden entry forcefully.

Giles clearly wanted no part of whatever this person and his oversized book were about and looked from one to the other as if they were of thin air. He continued his intended direction with a barely audible intake of breath.

"As I say, we're portioning a good deal of our operating funds to computerizing the regular holdings. Unfortunately—" he shifted his syrupy gaze to the hefty Texan "—as Rome wasn't built in a day..."

Basil Killingsley stepped back and craned his neck in disbelief. Cecil Blinn's attention on the heist was deflected by the import of the cliché: "Well, now I'm a feller who don't know a whole lot about liberries—

I'm from the school of hard knocks myself—but I'm no dummy. And I don't give money away to any ole thing. No sirree." Ceese was warming to his favorite topic: his own bootstraps. "The fact is my accountants tell me I gotta give more away, or Uncle Sam'll just grab more for himself."

Giles nodded in wise agreement and salaciously indicated that the Smedley would be delighted to assist him in his predicament.

"Well, sir," Cecil Blinn continued, rather more for the ears of all those present than his "sir" implied, "lemme lay my cards on the table and then I'd be obliged if you folks'ud do the same."

Giles and Sara nodded in rare unison and gestured for Blinn to continue. Basil remained standing, moving closer to the wall for a larger view of the whole baffling scene.

"My plan's like this: I want to know about everything around here. I want to know prices, salaries, costs—the whole kit and caboodle—and if stuff's gettin' heisted—" he winked good-naturedly at the professor "—so's I can decide how smooth this here operation is and where my money'll be goin'."

Giles Moraise controlled the alarm rising within his breast. He didn't need another pain in the ass, however much the Smedley needed the money. He grinned disingenuously, nodded agreeably, and tilted his chair back casually.

"Of course, of course, Ceese." He tapped the tips of his fingers together. A certain tenacity of purpose was in order.

"Well, I understand you'll be in town for a while so you'll have ample time to check out our, um, operations. I'll tell you what: tomorrow, why don't you get in touch with Dr. Tewksbury here—'' Giles bent a honeyed smile in Sara's direction "—and she'll set you on course. Perhaps we can have you—''

Plans for Cecil Blinn's itinerary were suddenly interrupted by disturbing cries moving down the hall from the circulation area toward the director's office.

"This is ridiculous, positively absurd!" Dr. Prout proclaimed for about the fifth time as he rounded the corner and strode through Giles Moraise's doorway. He was followed by Edwina Gluck, whose tentative wavings had no clear purport.

Oblivious of his interruption, Prout's penetrating eye pulled his neurasthenic person straight to Giles's desktop upon which lay the unwieldy volume of *The National Union Catalog*. He bent over it and his finger located the damned spot. For the sixth time, he fairly burst out: "This is ridiculous, positively absurd!"

Both Giles Moraise and Cecil Blinn were momentarily stunned by the inrush, though Giles gleaned disaster and Cecil, liberry operations. Sara Tewksbury, correctly assessing both the cause and the characters, stepped in to guide the situation. She nodded to Edwina Gluck and moved to relieve Dr. Prout of the volume with which Giles Moraise apparently wanted nothing to do.

"Oh, yes, Giles," she began in businesslike fashion, "I believe this is the reason we—the professor and I—came to see you in the first place."

"It is. It is indeed, Dr. Tewksbury," Basil Killingsley confirmed, thanking her with a nod and folding his hands over his slight paunch, feeling a shred of relief that perhaps a ray of sanity had returned. He rocked a bit on his heels and felt sufficiently vindicated to give Ms. Gluck a small, ambiguous nod.

Giles was caught between alleviating the situation, if only by hearing it through, and attempting to bury whatever fresh scandal this intrusive mob was fomenting.

"Um, perhaps, um, we can discuss the situation, um, later. We wouldn't want to detain our benefactor, Mr. Blinn, who I'm sure has dozens of more pressing concerns—"

"Who me? Nope. I got all day. Go right ahead. Spill the beans. I was just sayin' how's I should learn all about operations and I might as well start right in." He smiled around the group with great satisfaction. Only Sara and Basil returned his smile.

Giles closed his eyes briefly, pressed his fingers on the bridge of his nose, and resigned himself to spilled beans.

Sara continued. "It seems that Professor Killingsley was here several weeks ago—"

"Five, to be exact. Five weeks and two days. It was a Monday."

"Yes. He personally handled a Wynkyn de Worde fourteen ninety-five?" she queried and received Basil's approval, "edition of Ranulf Higden's *Polychronicon*."

Cecil Blinn appeared positively titillated.

"This afternoon he requested, from Ms. Gluck—" Sara acknowledged Ms. Gluck's presence in a way that thanked her for her years of service "—the same edition, but was informed that we have no such holding."

Ms. Gluck, hands folded over her groin, focused elsewhere to indicate her abdication of responsibility.

Giles Moraise silently moaned while Cecil Blinn's eyes were popping.

"Naturally the professor checked the card catalog and, to his surprise, there was no entry. Unfortunately, our rare books are not yet computerized," she casually added, watching Giles's glare sharpen, "except in crude numbers. In any event, the professor sought proof of the Smedley's possession of the Higden here in *The National Union Catalog*."

The volume was again placed on top of Giles's leather-tooled desk. He barely glanced at the page, while Cecil Blinn sidled to pore over it. Sara helped him locate the listing, and with her long maroon fingernail indicated the abbreviation for the Smedley.

"I told Professor Killingsley that we hadn't sold any incunabula since well before the catalog's publication in seventy-three, so I suggested we check with Dr. Prout."

"And that you did," Prout confirmed, acknowledging such wisdom with his deep-set, brooding eyes. He began his customary nervous peripatetics by pacing three feet away and then turning suddenly on his heel toward Moraise. His hands were clasped behind him and his shiny pate was bent slightly forward. Had Sherlock Holmes been bald, Prout would be a credible clone.

"At first I was quite calm, quite, quite calm and figured that some fool librarian—no offense, Ms. Gluck," he hastened to add, averting her shocked look, "that someone removed the entry card for whatever fool purposes. How many times do I have to announce that rare book entries, like the volumes themselves, are under *my* purview, and only *I* have authority for their removal?''

"That's true, Cyril. But tell us," Sara hastened to avert his egotistical foray, "was the Higden there?"

"No, Sara, it was not. However—" Prout resumed his short-run pacing, complete with manifest concentration on the Aubusson carpet underfoot "—there could be several reasons for its absence from the shelf; in any event, *that* is not the troublesome part. The troublesome part—the real conundrum—is that when I checked the shelf list—my private domain, I might add—the shelf card was not there!"

To all but Cecil Blinn the import of this revelation was indeed shocking. Seeing genuine concern pass over everyone's face, Ceese looked innocently from one to another.

"What Dr. Prout means, Ceese," Sara clarified, urged by a sense in the democratization of knowledge, "is that if there's no shelf card, it amounts to a person not having a birth certificate or any legal means of identification."

Prout rapidly bobbed his head in assent.

The director wanted nothing to do with a rehearsal of standard library practice and indicated such with a deep, bored sigh and renewed concentration on his twirling thumbs.

"The shelf cards," Sara continued with simple patience "—one for each item—are arranged in the order the items appear on each shelf." Cecil Blinn looked pleased at the common sense of the arrangement. "And once a year we hire college students to work as teams counting items and cards, and matching text to its card description. They go through the whole collection in a summer sweep."

"So's it's not enough for a body to swipe a book and that there card from the big catalog room? They gotta get themselves to the secret card so as not to be found out?"

"That's right. And the secret card contains complete bibliographic information and the market value at the time of purchase as well as the item's approximate worth for insurance purposes."

"Oh, I getcha," Cecil Blinn proudly announced. "So's nobody knows how much the stuff'ud bring in exceptin' this here feller?" Prout's head stopped its bobbing.

"More or less. Stolen books don't have quite the marketability of stolen cars or stereos." Sara spoke as if she regularly trafficked in hot merchandise.

"So's the guy who'd be doin' the rustlin' would have to be in the know—?"

"Excuse me," the director broke in. "Aren't we hastening to unwarranted conclusions? Short of this gentleman's—Professor Killingsley, is it?—short of your word," Giles shut his eyes to avoid being witness to Basil's evident umbrage, "and the *Union Catalog*, we really haven't much to go on."

Basil looked horrified. His glasses slipped down his nose by sheer propulsion from his glare.

"Professor Killingsley," Sara hastened to mollify, "Giles doesn't doubt your word, nor the indisputable evidence in the *Union Catalog*—"

"Ah, but it is," Cyril Prout added from out of nowhere.

"Is what?" Sara asked, beginning to feel like Alice in the rabbit hole.

"Is disputable."

Basil's sense of the horrific intensified. Though he logically knew that the *National Union Catalog* had not undergone the number of revisions and depth of textual scrutiny the Bible had, surely, he felt, they were in the same class of authority.

Prout continued, basking in the interest of his audience.

"Despite the teams of persons checking and verifying, errors do slip through. They do," he asserted, stopping in his tracks for emphasis. "Sometimes a SmD, our own abbreviation, might appear as capital SMD, which, of course, is ridiculous, or misread as SnD or countless other—"

"Yes, Cyril," Sara Tewksbury pleaded, "but the chance of such error is slim, and given Professor Killingsley's actual examination..."

Giles Moraise surreptitiously checked his wall clock, leaned forward, and picked up his pen to twirl nervously in his fleshy fingers. "Yes. Yes. Yes. Yes," he sighed with manifest boredom. "If we might just compose ourselves for a moment. Now, Dr. Prout, you say you have neither the—the—whatsits—"

"Higden. Ranulf Higden's *Polychronicon*, the fourteen—"

"Yes. Yes. The Higden. You have neither it nor its shelf card?"

"That is correct."

"Have you any knowledge as to its whereabouts or its existence?"

"I'm afraid not." Cyril Prout resumed his pacing and his recitation. "You see, when I joined the Smedley in January, I began a personal inventory in order to familiarize myself systematically with each and every item in the collection. Naturally," he appealed to no one in particular, "naturally I began at—well, one might say at the beginning, and as time and occasion permit, I examine a shelf or two." He paused in his peripatetics with hands still locked behind his back and gazed off into ceiling space, evidently reliving some of his finer moments at the Smedley.

"And did you inventory the Higden?" Giles Moraise asked, as much in the abstract interest of progress as in practical concern.

"No. You see," the pacing resumed, "I've only arrived at the eleven hundreds so I'm nowhere near Higden at—what is it?" Cyril darted to the *Union Catalog* where Basil still had his finger implanted. "Yes. The fifteen hundreds. I've miles to go before I'm there." Cyril paused and smiled at his faint poetic allusion.

Giles Moraise looked around and wondered how to get rid of the lot of them. Even Ms. Gluck, whose presence was as questionable here as elsewhere, was perplexed and had plastered herself against the wall opposite as if she were about to be frisked for the missing Higden. Giles's gaze narrowed to his assistant, signaling her not to open her damn mouth.

All eyes were on the director to direct. All, that is, except Basil's, whose had resumed scanning the *Union Catalog*.

"Good Lord! Oh, my, that's—of course! By George, that positively and irrefutably settles it," he murmured, pushing his glasses up his curved bridge and checking the catalog entry again. He was oblivious that his mutterings had become the central focus for the otherwise paralyzed group.

"You've found an error!" Cyril Prout hooted with barely disguised glee.

Basil looked up at the madman. "No, I have not found an *error*. I have found *confirmation* of my questioned veracity."

The group waited for Basil to go on. Even Cecil Blinn, beginning to suspect that there might be easier ways to give away money, was rapt in anticipation of the next screwy turn.

Another moment passed with the professor honing in on his find.

"Would you care to share your find with us?" Giles asked with caramelized patience.

Basil hadn't as much as paused in his "mmm-ing" and "yes-ing" under his breath. When he did, he looked up, removed his finger from the catalog, removed his glasses, and, in sum, reverted to his indigenous professorial posture.

"Five weeks ago when I examined the fourteen ninety-five Wynkyn de Worde edition of Ranulf Higden's *Polychronicon* right here in this very library," he spoke the prepositional phrase with subtle emphasis, "I was especially concerned with the quality of the musical notations—the first English printed example known, I might add. The musical notations, however, do not make the Smedley copy," again, Basil paused on the significant phrase, "unique, such being common to all copies of the de Worde fourteen ninety-five Higden. However, I failed to note, I did notice, but failed to assess as noteworthy," his bushy eyebrows flickered, "the unusual nature of the woodcut initials—the capital letters beginning a section, if you will." He glanced around to see if everyone was following. Everyone was, some like Giles with manifest annoyance, and some like Ceese with adolescent awe.

"They're by G. van Os." The professor waited for the import of his words to sink in.

He might have waited all day since no one present was a big G. van Os fan or had even heard of G. van Os, and therefore no one had the wit to be embarrassed at being caught in this hideous intellectual gap. Neither Edwina Gluck nor Cecil Blinn had a clue as to whether the woodcuts or the woodcutter were of significance; the Drs. Tewksbury and Prout were a bit more sophisticated and recognized where the professor had placed his emphasis. Giles Moraise was beyond caring.

"And the G. van Os woodcut initials appear only in…?" Sara Tewksbury trailed off, hoping not to step into some other gaffe that would set Basil Killingsley off in uncharted directions.

"Precisely, Dr. Tewksbury. Precisely." Sara's stock was rising higher in the professor's eyes. "They appear in very few—*very* few—perhaps two or three extant editions of fourteen ninety-five Higden. One speculates that de Worde had acquired them just as he was doing a last runoff. He'll use them—in fact, he'll use *all* G. van Os type the next year in his reprint of the *Book of St. Albans*, which, of course, distinguishes itself in bibliographic annals as—"

"As containing a chapter on fishing with an angle!" Cyril Prout announced triumphantly, delighted to redeem himself from the pit of G. van Os ignorance.

"Ah, good for you, old chap! So few take note of bibliographic landmarks these days." Basil Killingsley was heartened by the unexpected discovery of a fellow traveler and might have gone on to invite Cyril Prout for a sherry had not Sara Tewksbury channeled the flow.

"And as for these two or three extant Higdens with G. van Os woodcuts—"

"Ah, my, yes. I say two or three because I'm certain that there's only one in the United States, and one in England, but there may be another abroad. *One,* mind you, in our homeland. And that *one,* gentlemen, ladies," he bowed ever so slightly to each in turn, "was right here in the Smedley five weeks ago!"

Cecil Blinn was not alone in thinking that they were back to square one. Basil, however, read their blank stares as collective awe and resumed only when he felt the wave of interest cresting.

"So naturally you all see that I couldn't have been mistaken—as my wife suggested—and examined the Higden at some other library. I saw the G. van Os initials and I saw them *here!*"

The significance of G. van Os, having been made manifest to the thickest of the group, forced Giles to return from his world beyond care.

"Well, er, yes, Professor. Er...we see what you mean..." He stumbled. "Um...however, it may well be that what we have here is a case of, er...um...a misplaced volume—and we'll initiate search procedures first thing tomorrow—"

"Excuse me, but the entry card and the shelf card..." Cyril Prout's unraised index finger underlined the irrefutable evidence of deliberate and unauthorized removal of the text, a.k.a. theft.

Whereas he had entered Moraise's office expecting some logical explanation, if not Giles himself to whip out the Higden from his top drawer, he now felt the anguish of a parent whose child is missing.

"The Higden—a rare Higden, as this gentleman so keenly observed—plus the Hilton *Scala Perfecconis* and the *Eneydos*—"

"Dr. Prout..." Giles spoke sternly, attempting to stem the catalog of loss.

Cyril was too moved by his litany to heed the director's warning.

"My God," he went on, hypnotized by the thought, "Davies's masterful work, his *Sovereigne salve to cure the worlds madness*—gone! That irreplaceable watershed in sixteenth-century psychoses!"

Basil Killingsley, though not the only one to appreciate the extent of damage being chronicled, moved to put his hand on the crushed curator's shoulder.

For Giles, Sara, and Ms. Gluck, the recent hushed-up losses meant serious blows to the Smedley's modest but nonetheless international reputation. For the likes of the Drs. Prout and Killingsley, however, the losses went beyond matters of prestige: family and friends had been filched. For Cecil Blinn, who was groping to make sense of books you couldn't read, the losses nonetheless registered significance in dollars and cents.

Cyril Prout gratefully acknowledged Basil's compassionate gesture while Giles Moraise, not about to put up with slobbering sentimentality advertising dubious security measures, marshaled his directional starch.

"Dr. Prout, this is indeed serious. But we must not become hysterical and race about like silly schoolgirls—"

"Children," Sara interposed.

"Huh? Oh, dammit, Tewksbury..." He shut his eyes and reglued himself. "Like silly school*children*. There is one other avenue to be investigated before assuming theft, and that is to check with Leon Boehm."

Again, Sara Tewksbury briefly explained that Mr. Boehm, the Smedley auditor, was the final means of inventory accountability. He kept track of all supplies, merchandise, personnel, salaries, and, yes, books bought, sold, ditched, or traded.

"Or heisted," Cecil added.

"Yes. Or heisted," Sara concluded, dropping her arms and bangling her beads. No dummy he, she thought.

THREE

BASIL KILLINGSLEY and Cyril Prout were of one sad mind as they left the director's office. The professor, sensitive to such matters, knew better than to drill poor Dr. Prout on the Smedley rare book losses he had let slip moments before. As curator of a thinning collection, as indeed a Rachel figure lamenting children lost, Cyril Prout undoubtedly could not easily be snatched from the black hole of despair into which he was being sucked.

Still clutching the hefty *Union Catalog*, Basil drifted into the reading room, despite Miss Sisson's tiny yelps and frantic gestures from down the hall at reference. He was unready to part with his irrefutable evidence lest it, too, be swallowed up by God knew what. And perhaps further examination might reveal some clue. He slumped down at a small reading desk and gazed off into bibliographic space. Only the quiet—one might say stealthy—movement of that little prim lady ruffled Basil's comatose stare. His mind registered vague familiarity.

The figure belonged to Edna Leddy, sixty-two, widowed, and a regular Smedley fixture. Each day she would appear at precisely 9:15 A.M., nod to old Cribbs, the kindly, but useless security officer, and go about her nonsalaried business of roving in the stacks and reading rooms. Everyone on the Smedley staff was familiar with her white gloves, genteel hat, and navy blue string bag. Edna herself hadn't a clue as to her popularity; she assumed that by keeping her torso tilted to book spines, touching little, and looking squarely at no one, she could go about her days in happy anomie.

Unfortunately, her placid foraging had this day been disrupted, Basil noted, by a lanky, baggy-trousered fellow she seemed to be stalking. The professor, by now sensitized to the enigmatic in the Smedley, watched the surreptitious trailing. The tall, gaily suspendered fellow was scanning the shelves in the second archive while Edna Leddy was scanning him from between shelf space in the first archive. (Was she his mother? Basil wondered.) Suddenly the lanky fellow's progress halted as he happily latched upon a volume, opened it, and nodded. He snapped the book shut, tucked it under his arm, looked about innocently, and resumed his scanning. Basil, not wishing to appear a snooper, had forced his eyeballs back to the *Union Catalog* page. The fellow, breathily whistling, rounded the corner to the third archive and again looked about for witnesses. Apparently confident that the frizzy-haired character poring over the huge tome at the small table by the windows was engrossed in his dull matter, the lanky fellow turned and slipped his chosen volume into his generous trouser pocket.

Edna Leddy's gloved hand silenced a horrified gasp, and Basil screwed up his gooseberry eyes. The volume that had been tucked under that loping fellow's arm was no longer tucked, and there was a squarish bulge in his left trouser pocket.

While Basil Killingsley had more practical sense than to tackle the alleged thief (he knew the precarious posture of the law as well as the limitations of his physical stamina), he was convinced that no one—not even the cocky fellow—could be so stupid with regard to library security. He would surely be caught at the door.

Edna Leddy, on the other hand, had no such confidence. The pocketing of the volume was not the first irregularity Edna's vigilant eye had spotted, but it was the first indisputably illegal one. She had seen the occasional pen quietly dash across margins of library material (surely a serious offense, but how she so enjoyed reading anonymous marginalia); she had witnessed the coupon clippers snipping away in the few popular magazines to which the Smedley subscribed, and was herself tempted to save a few cents on cat food; and certainly she heard the breakage of book spines by overzealous patrons attempting to flatten reading pages. None of these misdemeanors, however, held a candle to outright theft. She would have to do something, but what? Tell that Ms. Gluck at circulation? Ms. Gluck, it was clear, thought her a daffy old biddy. Edna had caught her more than once denying the availability of some book that Edna knew very well was right on the shelf where it was supposed to be. No. She would not go to Ms. Gluck.

The light from the east windows of the reading room where Basil sat was beginning to fade. The professor accepted the pathetic fallacy of nature's congruence with his darkening mood. He rose, carting volume 245 of *The National Union Catalog* in both arms. Perhaps he ought to alert the authorities, he thought, recalling the assistant director's remarks about inadequate security, to say nothing of his own proof of it furnished by the missing Higden. No need to be dramatic, making a citizen's arrest or causing a stir; a mere word to...to...? Basil had reentered the lobby weighted by his various burdens and pondering alternatives.

Winifred Sisson, who hadn't moved from the reference room threshold in order to keep one eye in and one out on the lookout for the purloined volume for which she felt personally responsible, emitted a tiny yet audible shriek when she spotted it cradled in the thief's arms.

Ms. Gluck, on her way to her station, glared as if something terribly sexual had happened.

Basil moved toward the trembling arms of Miss Sisson, who was straining her torso to regain her property a second sooner. Her elongation and nervous flapping suggested something of a bird with trapped feet attempting flight.

Cecil Blinn, oblivious to the subtleties around him, was trailing Sara Tewksbury as the principal provider of insights into library operations.

"Where does this here Berm feller hang out?" he asked, hoping to get on with the matter.

Sara liked Ceese's directness. She tentatively considered introducing him to Save Venice from Sinking, but only if he gave up on the Smedley. Before, however, she could appropriate a dime for any cause, a distracted figure in a pink alligator shirt athletically strode up the grand staircase.

At the juncture of the stairs and lobby area, Hortense Killingsley flitted left, then right, searching the

walls and ceilings until her focus settled on the person
of Sara Tewksbury.

"Dr. Tewksbury, oh, good. I'm afraid Basil's disappeared again. Lost in library space!" She spoke as
if Sara were long familiar with Basil's spatial disloca-
tions. "You know he was once locked overnight in the
Newberry?" She turned to Cecil Blinn as if he, too,
would be interested. "Thank goodness a security officer and not Doberman pinschers found him. Reading away in a carrel as if—oh, sorry! I'm being
tedious." She looked at Cecil and made mental note.
"Oh, yes, Basil. I've come to prevent another of his
innocent incarcerations, grand old place as the Smedley is," she dithered on, clutching her wood-handled
purse to her bosom and admiring the marbled corn-
ices. "Quite Palladian."

Sara smiled at Hortense's love of fine old things like
the library and Basil.

"Don't worry. Your husband's safe and visible in
the reference room—"

"I should have guessed; he takes in catalogs the way
perverts do pornography."

Cecil Blinn chuckled. He was enjoying the company of tall women.

Ms. Gluck glowered with sufficient force to quell
Hortense's amplified chatter.

"My, yes. We're disturbing things around here. If I
might just retrieve my wayward husband...ah, there.
Basil! Yoo-hoo, Basil..." she chimed in dulcet tones
to Ms. Gluck's evident, but unnoticed dismay.

Basil, once again in his realm, was engaged in explaining the Higden situation to Miss Sisson, whom he
assumed was desperate to know full details. She was

not. However, as indifference never quite registered with the professor, he burbled on, pointing and page-turning with great absorption. Hortense walked over to rescue poor, bullied Winifred.

"What gave me the clue was this," Basil's finger was virtually boring a hole in the page. Miss Sisson glanced down and smiled feebly, hoping he wasn't violent.

"Basil, are you coming home this evening? If not, I'll have to discard the cod, as it was nearly cooked in the car."

"My dear, I was just informing this young woman—Miss Sisson, I believe?—of my discovery that the Smedley's Higden—"

"You found it!" Hortense whooped uncontrollably. Ms. Gluck rose from her stool, ready to call in the National Guard.

"My dear, do let me finish. No, I did not find it. I found that the Smedley's copy is one—one of two or three extant—with G. van Os initials."

The significance of this morsel was not wasted on Hortense. The reckless enthusiasm of the couple over G. van Os was more than Ms. Gluck could professionally tolerate. Her sacred adherence to library regulations would not be mocked. Even Sara Tewksbury and Cecil Blinn, still in the central lobby, were drawn to the commotion.

"You sure as hell get worked up over that old—that incunabula book," Cecil Blinn chided Basil good-naturedly, pleased at his pronunciation.

"My dear man . . . Mr. Blinn, is it?"

"Ceese to my friends."

Basil unconsciously craned his neck forward to get a better look at this specimen.

"Yes, Ceese. The volume in question is worth quite a bit." This time Basil knew his audience. "Probably somewhere in the neighborhood of one or two thousand dollars—if it's as complete and undoctored as I believe."

It was Cecil's turn to examine a specimen. "That's all? One or two G's?"

"Ah, but—Ceese, may I—?" Hortense burst in as Ms. Gluck stormed over to the group with fire in her beady eyes. She fiercely tapped a skinny finger to her pursed lips and aggressively marched on as if pretending not to have the runs.

Hortense lowered her voice. "It's not the monetary worth; it's the—"

"Right, ma'am. This here Mizz Tewksbury's been tellin' me all about that. Why, hell, I could buy you a roomful of them there Higdens."

The extent of Mr. Blinn's potential generosity did not go unregistered with the Smedley's assistant director.

"Say," the benefactor rushed on in friendly Texan fashion, "Mizz Tewksbury here and me were just about to take ourselves on a little tour and maybe check out the auditor feller. Maybe you should come along to give the lowdown?"

Though it was after quitting time for the administrative staff, the vision of a roomful of Higdens encouraged Sara's indulgence. Besides, Ceese was a genuine article, and both Ms. Gluck and Miss Sisson could profit from this congeries' absence.

Basil was happy for any activity that would forward his mission and Hortense knew better than to impede his path. Besides, her own curiosity took precedence over rotting codfish.

As they all trundled down four levels to the basement, through the dusty Cutter book drawers, Basil lectured a fascinated Ceese on outmoded library classification systems and Hortense explained something of herself to Sara. Every few seconds she'd check on her husband who, she feared, was liable to get sucked into one of the musty rows of sliding shelves.

"They really aren't worth much." Basil was expanding on his topic. "Cutter clutter," he chuckled. "Most of it's dreadfully outdated or somewhere in the intellectual vicinity of the Hardy Boys."

Not much of Basil's lecture registered with Cecil Blinn, but it was too dark for anyone to notice his vaguely puzzled expression. And, besides, Hortense filled the air with her own chatty obscurities.

"What chronically irks me is that Adelaide Phillpotts was relegated to just such dustbins well before her less gifted brother Eden. And he's *still* in the stacks in some places!" She halted and looked straight at Sara, expecting a show of feminist solidarity.

Cecil Blinn, looking about in the dim light for what clarification the locale might reveal on the Phillpotts siblings, rammed right into the women.

"Whoops, sorry, ma'am," he blurted.

Sara reached over to the shelf end and switched on another section of lights. Not far down the aisle, in the corner of the dingy basement, they could see a frosted glass cage, the home of the Smedley internal auditor, Leon Boehm. The door was ajar.

Mr. Boehm was seated in his small cubicle, which was largely filled with file cabinets and computer equipment. He had on Dickensian eyeshades to cut the fluorescent glare on the piles of green and white computer printouts covering every surface.

Sara tapped on the door lintel. Leon Boehm didn't stir in his swivel chair, seemingly mesmerized by his columns and figures. Sara knocked more forcefully. Still nothing from Boehm.

"Perhaps he's asleep," Hortense whispered. "I know I nod off juggling my checkbook, and I'm comatose with the taxes, isn't that so, Basil?"

Basil stepped past Sara toward the slumped figure. He touched him gently on the shoulder. Leon slowly moved forward until his head clunked on the desk.

"Oh," Hortense emitted, recognizing the possible permanency of the auditor's condition.

Basil felt for a pulse as Sara and Ceese rushed in to offer superfluous aid. Hortense searched for her purse mirror and pressed it to Leon's face.

"I'm afraid he's quite gone," she declared. "Even his body is chill. Basil, you're better at the signs of rigor mortis..."

"Yes. I'd say he's been dead for a day or two. Let's not touch anything," Basil sensibly warned just as Sara was about to pick up the phone.

"There's no blood," Hortense reflected, peering around Leon's body. "Poison? Strangulation? Fright?"

"Dear, you're favoring the insidious. People do die quite often on their own steam."

Hortense dismissed the dull fact even before she noticed the thin multicolored cable beside the body.

"Aha, strangled by a computer cable, see here." She indicated the item by caricatured gesture rather than by touch.

Sara gave a "good God" look and turned to go. "I'll be back in a minute. Ceese, unless you want to get involved with a mess of questions, you'd be wise to cut out now."

"Me? Nope, I'm with you. I never knew liberry operations got so serious. Who d'ya suppose'd want to kill an auditor?" he asked, evidently adopting Hortense's hypothesis.

"You and I are getting out of here. You, out of the building, me to phone the authorities."

With a bit more room in the rabbit warren office, Hortense and Basil examined surfaces, craning their necks for more intense scrutiny of the papers and auditing paraphernalia lying messily about. Hortense was bent over the corpse trying to read what was under Leon Boehm's head when a knock rattled the door. She started, and instinctively her hand upraised to her mouth, on the way to which it grazed the body, shifting it a few inches. She gasped. Basil silently shushed her and opened the door a crack.

"Thank you, but I believe Mr. Boehm is indisposed at the moment and, um," Basil looked around the inner room convincingly, "he doesn't seem to have an abundance of trash. Thanks, anyway." He quickly shut the door and turned back to scanning surfaces.

"Look, Basil, there's a rather horrid letter here. I'm not touching a thing, but see here: 'Incompetent, untrustworthy, mechanical cruncher; total lack of sensitivity to institutional values. Treats library material as so many sacks of potatoes without regard to intan-

gible, intrinsic worth.'" Hortense's head was nearly
upside down trying to decipher the rest. "There's
more, but I can only—" Her itching fingers tugged at
the tiniest portion of the corner of the letter. "Ah,
'something...um...accountant...um, cannot be
trusted to water potted plants.' My goodness, apparently Mr. Boehm was not a favored Smedley em-
ployee. 'Rating: zero.' It's signed by Mr. Moraise."

"Placement of such incriminating evidence does
appear to weigh against Mr. Moraise being the murderer."

"Nonsense. Mr. Moraise may well have planted the
incriminating evidence to capitalize on reverse psy-
chology."

Basil was too absorbed in decipherment of his own
to acknowledge his wife's devious reasoning.

"Look here. Account number o nine one, two eight
seven nine, rare books. Let me see, ah, yes, a standard spreadsheet arrangement. Scarcely very sophisticated for an institution of this sort, but as that tall
Dr. Tewksbury confirmed, librarians tend to be among
the last to concede to technological advances. It took
centuries for the abacus to catch on in Alexandria. Let
me see. Mmm." Basil nudged his glasses to the bridge
of his nose and pored over the document. "Ah, I see.
Dear, look at this a moment."

Hortense broke away from the letter beneath the
body and focused her attention over Basil's shoulder.
"Looks like quarterly tallies. By—good Lord!—by
call number groups? That does place books on par
with potatoes. 001 to 100: 83, 83, 79...the first col-
umn in bold is probably last summer's tally—you
know, the sweep Dr. Tewksbury was telling me about.

So then this is fall, and the third's winter—down four—'' Basil's eyes scanned the sheet. He turned it over to continue down until he came to the 1501–1600 line. He carefully read the quarterly numbers across.

Hortense, meanwhile, having mastered the primitive accounting schema herself, moved on to study the pile of computer printouts on the top of a file cabinet. "You know, Basil, I can't decide if they run a very careless ship around here or what. According to this, over the course of the last three quarters the Smedley's down fourteen swivel chairs. At four hundred and fifty dollars each. Goodness, you can get perfectly decent ones at Discount City for half that. Would you believe," she continued, unfolding back the pages, "last year a worse story yet: down seventeen. What do you suppose librarians do to wear out swivel chairs?''

"A hundred seventeen last summer, a hundred seventeen in the fall, a hundred seventeen winter, and a hundred twelve for the spring.''

"A hundred twelve what, dear?''

"Down five rare books in the fifteen oh one to sixteen hundred range—largely incunabula, I suspect. That's very odd given Dr. Tewksbury's testimony that no rare books have been sold or whatever in years.''

"Hmm. They're holding their own in desk blotters and light fixtures . . .''

"And this can't be including the absent Higden.''

RELUCTANT AS SHE WAS to abandon Basil with the body (and the equally frightening tally sheets), Hortense felt compelled to report the irregularities to the Smedley officials lest the police latch on first and catch the administration unawares. Considering her size vis-à-vis the stack stairwell's, she deftly maneuvered herself up the four levels and simultaneously caught her breath at the sight of Sara Tewksbury in the lobby. The assistant director had just shuffled Cecil Blinn out the door with the promise of exchanging lowdown for dinner.

"Oh, good! Dr. Tewksbury." Hortense flapped at her generous bosom with the hand not clutching her mashed purse.

"Yes, Professor Killingsley. Have you discovered another body? Or has the one discovered become mobile?"

"No, no—though I'm all in favor of life after death."

Ms. Gluck, whose perceptive ears missed no intimacy in the Smedley, jutted forward at the mention of bodies. Sara caught the startled move and saw need to temper Ms. Gluck's rush to the insidious with a dose of fact. The circulation librarian looked elsewhere at the approach of the assistant director and Hortense Killingsley.

"Ms. Gluck," Sara spoke, leaning over the counter, "I don't think this should be broadcast, but there's been a terrible accident and Mr. Boehm is dead in his office."

Edwina lurched and grabbed her bony throat. "Dead?" she blurted.

"Shh." Sara took small pleasure in silencing the Smedley silence enforcer.

"The authorities are going to be traipsing through shortly so give them full cooperation."

"Are you certain—he's dead?"

"Yes. You know, inert, cold, no vital signs, that sort of thing..."

"I'll second that," Hortense confirmed. "And my husband Basil—who is rarely mistaken—has established the onset of rigor mortis." She nodded with satisfaction.

Ms. Gluck looked annoyed, but her native curiosity overcame her. "Murdered?"

Hortense's eyes lit up, not so much in finding a compatriot in the sinister as in suspecting Ms. Gluck herself who, after all, hadn't a clue (or so she feigned) and yet leapt to judgment.

Sara wondered why foul play was everyone's immediate conclusion, especially as Leon had kept himself pretty much squirreled away in the basement. She shrugged her shoulders and turned to leave, bumping into Hortense, who maintained rigid fixation on the potential felon. The jolt triggered a second thought in the assistant director's brain.

"Oh, yes, Ms. Gluck, I wonder if you'd be good enough to locate Herman Lobel?"

"Who?"

"Mr. Boehm's assistant, Herman Lobel?"

Ms. Gluck's blank stare turned quizzical. "He had an assistant?"

"Only for the last four years. Pudgy fellow—twenty-five going on sixty? Bad case of acne...?"

Not a shred of recognition registered on Edwina Gluck's face. "Are you certain?"

It was Sara's turn for exasperation. "Never mind, I'll find him myself."

Sara and Hortense turned in unison and marched purposefully down the hall on rubber-soled feet. Sara's purpose was to inform her boss and the police; Hortense's was to align herself with truth and to rescue her beloved spouse from the body watch.

Only the jangle of Sara Tewksbury's African ornaments alerted Giles Moraise to the purposeful women's approach.

FOUR

WHEN SARA REPORTED the condition of Leon Boehm to her boss, he chose to treat her tale as typical Tewksbury histrionics.

"Dr. Tewksbury, unless you're off to Afghanistan to monitor their toothpick supply, as my assistant I give you full permission to clean up the bloody mess."

"There's no blood," Hortense asserted in the interests of truth. She was about to unravel her own theory of probable cause, but Giles was evidently unreceptive to her sleuthing skills.

"How nice to hear we won't have to hose down Mr. Boehm's office. Nevertheless, surely, Dr. Tewksbury, you can handle the police while I compose some appropriate public statement? I can't pretend to feel great loss at Mr. Boehm's demise as he was not the most efficient of auditors. His death on Smedley premises only attests to that." Giles picked up an auction catalog and continued reading where he left off.

Hortense, for the second time in as many minutes, felt her detectional dudgeon rise. Not only was that supposed professional librarian, that dour Ms. Gluck, collecting suspicions about her, but here was the head of the entire institution, the very director himself, pulling quite the *noli me tangere* act when evidence as rife as his evaluation letter of Mr. Boehm lay beneath the deceased begging for the long arm of the law to reach out and finger the author. However, Hortense also knew that to reveal too much too soon might well forewarn the guilty. She therefore chose to continue in her role as casual, nay, nonchalant witness while Sara Tewksbury phoned the police.

The buxom scholar-detective, almost breaking into a hum, surveyed the office walls. Her eyes, however, were in the far corners of their sockets in order to glean the state of the director's swivel chair. A very high quality one, she thought, not the sort available at Discount City. Probably close to a thousand dollars with its brass tacking and mahogany frame. Well, she self-satisfyingly crossed off an item on her mental list, we can rule out this fellow's complicity in the appalling swivel chair tallies. Even a $450 version wouldn't do for someone into, my, yes, genuine Aubusson underfoot. Hortense's eyes continued their innocent sweep. Giles Moraise rattled his catalog to indicate his preference for solitude.

"Ah, Mr. Moraise," Hortense cheerily worked up her literary interest, "are you thinking of purchasing," she tilted a bit toward the opened catalog to catch a title or two, "a, um, Emerson? Wonderful essayist, don't you think? Did his share in shaping our mother tongue..."

Giles Moraise looked at Hortense Killingsley with the disdain he usually reserved for his assistant, who was toying with a gruesome *objet* dangling from her ear while waiting for the police on the other end of the line to draw straws for the Smedley assignment.

"Yes, um..." he entuned half-heartedly, groping for the irritant's name.

"Hortense Killingsley. Dr., Professor, Ms.—though one could include Mrs. as Basil—the fellow who's found the Higden missing?—yes, Basil's mine."

"How splendid for the two of you, I'm sure," Giles responded, raising his dark eyebrows over his glasses, but not removing his eyeballs from the catalog page.

"Neither of us is an Americanist, though we might get there someday given longevity..."

Giles looked squarely at the babbler.

"And we have made minor inroads—what with Webster for me and mercantilism for Basil."

Sara, still hanging on to the phone, had one hip on Giles's desk edge. Her tapping fingernails ceased with a renewed rattle of the catalog and Giles's deep sigh of annoyance. To maintain his sanity, he focused on the lesser of the two obnoxious women with whom he could at least follow his own fancy.

"Yes, Mrs.—Professor Killingsley. I am considering bolstering our Americana collection."

Sara's ears perked. It was the first she'd heard of the plan.

"I daresay that's a good idea given the Smedley's geographical location—" Hortense said agreeably.

Giles perked up. It was the only sensible thing he heard the woman say. "Indeed, just my thought. Americana for the Americans. New Englanders for New England!"

Sara Tewksbury turned away as much to conceal her puzzlement as to respond to the life reviving at the other end of the phone line. She finished giving what information she could, hung up, and ushered a reluctant would-be patriot out the director's door before another wave of the flag swept them out.

The police, having taken Sara's word that the party in question was in fact dead, took their time arriving at the scene, which was all to the good in terms of minimizing disruption to the late-afternoon browsers. On the other hand, Sara hoped they'd be quick enough to get there before decomposition.

Meanwhile, Basil Killingsley, having relieved himself from the pointless body watch, met the assistant director as she was suggesting to his wife that they remain on the premises for questioning.

"Well, there certainly are enough questions lurking about, aren't there?" Hortense asserted. "You do know about the rare book tallies? Basil's hasty check of Mr. Boehm's cabbage count revealed a decided decline—"

"Indeed," Basil corroborated, explaining his sample examination of the 1501–1600 range. "Down five for the spring. Plus the Higden."

Sara sighed. "Yes, I know. But the odd thing—or odder, I should say—is that the summer sweep is revealing something of a reversal of the downward trend. There's really no accounting for the losses or gains. We should always be stable."

"So true," Basil responded to what he read as sound general advice. "Ah, well, my dear," he continued to his wife, "let's not waste precious library time in idle speculation. We might as well carry on normally until the police arrive."

It wasn't easy, however, for either Killingsley to carry on normally, but Basil, as a historian of latitudinarian tendencies, was going to give it his best shot by pursuing in the reading room the effects of William the Conqueror's victory in 1066 (as opposed to

either Harold's) on Britain's later imperialistic policies, while Hortense figured to wrench some revelation from the medieval stacks.

Unlike her more restrained husband who was content quietly to amass facts, findings, and specula-
tions, allowing them mature issuance in publication,
Hortense could master no such restraint. As a linguist
of the broad school (was not all that which was expressed in language under the linguist's purview?), she
couldn't resist bursting forth to anyone within ear's
reach. Fellow stack-hunters, librarians, efficient jani-
tors—each and all might at some time serve as target
for inquiry. Who knew (she'd ask the unwary), who
knew where Taglog truly fit into the scheme of things?
The Smedley janitor, Barney Dibbs, had already been
privy to the fact that in all cases thus far sampled, an-
cient Luwian did follow the P > B drift, though,
Hortense meticulously noted, there was no solid evidence to demonstrate that T drifted to D in any environment, or that diphthongization by initial palatals
had ever been a live option for the Luwanese.

"Nonetheless, a connection—something beginning
to shape itself into a linguistic pattern—does exist,"
she had convinced Barney Dibbs without much opposition.

"Ye dinna sae?" he had assented politely, and continued to wave his feather duster over the shelves.

The encounter Hortense struck up this day within
minutes of leaving the director's environs was with the
summer sweepers, the dozens of odd student teams on
their rampage through the shelves checking book
against card and card against book, recording every
discrepancy with what was for most, inordinate care.

Though the workers variously dealt with the problems of removed and shifted material (the more feckless frankly ignoring those minor currents of change), few could resist the disruptions engendered by the likes of Hortense Killingsley, who, through irrepressible need to share her finds and proselytize her minority views, constituted an abnormal source of interference for the eager tally-takers in the cool, dim stacks.

"Ah yes, a C version of *Piers Plowman*!" she exclaimed to an unsuspecting tally-taker, filching the volume from his hand. "Do you know that the Northwest Midlands dialect, here amply represented, shows a decided advance in instances of yogh to H or G (given different palatal needs) over the B version? And heaven knows how far things have gone from the A version!"

This particular team of students working the PR 2000s smiled weakly.

"You realize, of course," she continued, carefully perusing the pages and then looking point-blank at the intimidated team, "they do teach you about such things—medieval literature, you know, Chaucer, the Gawain-Poet...?" her voice trailed off anticipating a response.

"Er...I, er, guess. I had Chaucer," one student began, recognizing some distantly familiar ground.

"Then it shouldn't come as news to you that, based on the single fact of yogh density, some speculate A, B, and C by different hands?"

The student was caught between revealing the depth of his undergraduate ignorance and retrieving PR 2010/P4/1979 from the woman's clutches so it might be appropriately tallied.

Hortense, however, gave no sign of yielding the volume. In fact, her perusal, not being interrupted by any significant phonemic contribution from the students, deepened, and within moments she was mentally in the Malvern Hills lulled by the alliterative sibilants, liquids, and resonating nasals.

The team, both the accosted member and his partner several feet away, shrugged and went on to the next card and volume. Their tacit agreement was to count PR 2010/PR/1979 as missing.

Meanwhile, Basil Killingsley's attention, ostensibly directed toward clues linking William the Conqueror and Benjamin Disraeli, was caught by another, more evasive Victorian. It was that same lady again darting between and around the archives, suspiciously straining to appear innocent.

When Edna Leddy ruled out revealing to Ms. Gluck the theft of the small volume, she went back to the reading room to sort out a plan. Evidently the baggy-trousered culprit had removed himself along with his loot, so there was no rush to report the matter. But she had been keeping her eyes peeled for unwarranted spaces on the shelves.

Basil, reminded of the earlier incident this lady's stealth had revealed, sighed as much for his absent-mindedness in reporting the matter as for the renewed distraction she represented. He deliberately turned his head, noted, and nodded to Michel Farb who was seated at his regular station in the same wing chair he sat in every day at precisely four o'clock. The Frenchman prided himself on regularity, which he aligned with stability and prosperity. These were qualities that made him a successful banker and esteemed chair-

man of the board for the Smedley. He nodded to Basil
Killingsley and, as she rounded the corner of the
fourth archive, to Edna Leddy over the journal he read
each day at that time—woe to the innocent who might
unfold *Le Monde* before him. Edna acknowledged
M. Farb's greeting and kept moving in her overly
innocuous manner to the far end of the alcove where
the tall wooden alleys afforded familiar stillness and
invisibility. She slipped into the DA 100s–DQ 200s and
took up scanning book spines. Basil, in the next alcove over among the HTs, noted Edna's avoidance of
eye contact. (That, his wife Hortense maintained, always signaled suspicion, if not outright guilt.) Several
moments into her mechanical gazing, somewhere
above the multivolumed *Works of W. D. Prescott*
(specifically the one on Ferdinand and Isabella) Edna's eye spotted Herman Lobel in the adjacent alcove
opposite to where the scattered white-haired profes-
sor-sort was spying. This fellow, the pimply youth,
was lurking about with an armload of books. Basil
could make out only the fellow's back and the fact
that it was generating inordinate interest for the old
lady. Edna, who was now peering through the DQ
110–200 shelf, followed the back and the head that
now and again darted a look as if to check on security. He was not by Edna's accounts a regular, and
certainly not a librarian (much too pudgy and ill-
kempt); therefore, she convinced herself, here was
another thief, and this time she would do her duty as
a loyal Smedley patron and civic-minded person: she
would make a citizen's arrest.

What saved Edna from rushing forth to bind the
person of Herman Lobel legally was the fact that

Herman was not removing books from shelves and
tucking them into his underwear. No, Edna, and then
Basil noted, he was putting books *on* shelves, even
where it meant rearranging books from one shelf to
another to make room.

Basil recalled the shelf-stuffer as the bungling youth
with whom he collided an hour or so ago, and here he
was with his armload of books. Although he hoped to
catch sight of a title or two from the fellow's batch to
corroborate or dismiss the Tottel nonsense, he was
curious about the lurking little old lady. Was she his
mother?

Edna watched where Herman placed what volumes
and, holding her gaze steady, she waited for him to
move on until she could prudently snatch the very
book. Basil watched Edna watch Herman. Hanging
on to an edition of *The Anglo-Saxon Chronicle* as a
cover, he moved down to the end of his alcove just as
Edna was reaching the end of hers, but being attentive to her prey, she didn't notice the professor's quiet
movement. She moved into the BA 100–CT 300 alcove (the one vacated by Herman) as Basil moved into
the DA 100–DQ 200 alley that Edna just left. As if
drawn by a magnet, Edna Leddy zeroed in on several
volumes.

Oddly, as best as Basil could see from his skewered
vantage, the several volumes she had thus plucked
were all entitled *Songs and Sonnets Written by the
Right Honourable Lord Henry Haward Late Earl of
Surrey and Other*. There were different editions—
some new, some old, but all with the same title, par-
enthetically and otherwise identified as Tottel's *Miscellany*. Though it struck each of them as odd that the

Smedley should be purchasing—well, as far as they knew, upward of a dozen of the same thing, what was even odder was that virtually the same title was variously numbered and placed. There was a Tottel's *Miscellany* alongside the works of Michel Foucault; another beside Theodore Roszak; another in the vicinity of René Dubos; and Karl Marx had his Tottel tucked in beside.

Basil had followed Edna who had followed Herman from the BAs to the HQs to the RBs. Wherever he inserted a volume, she riveted her eyeballs, waited, and plucked. After five or six of these furtive ventures, she decided to keep track by jotting down the call numbers of the many *Songs and Sonnets*. When Herman had run out of his armload, Basil followed Edna as she scurried off to the card catalog.

Basil was now certain that he was not a victim of Hortense's contagious overactive imagination. Though he was seeing an enigmatic world in every grain of sand, such were the grains. He decided to sidle up to the P card files as Edna clucked and shook her head at the S drawer cards. Basil's upraised, scattered brows gazed over to the *Songs and Sonnets* entries engendering the woman's clucks, while his fingers innocently plied the few *Polychronicon* references.

The prim lady, having gathered what information she had sought, stiffened in search of someone of authority. To maintain his inconspicuous status, Basil propelled his head into the Poly-Pron drawer with such force that his reading glasses fell to the floor. Meanwhile, the elderly investigator was gathering her indignation to approach the circulation desk and the person of Ms. Gluck. There simply was no one else.

From his fortuitous cover among the furniture legs and on all fours in search of his spectacles, Basil Killingsley watched the curious exchange of the two women.

"Yes, I understand, Ms. Leddy, but—"

"*Mrs.* Ian died nearly a decade ago."

"Sorry, *Mrs.* Leddy, I'm afraid you must be mistaken. No one of that description works here and I can't imagine a thief of such generous nature."

"I tell you I saw him put the unauthorized books on the shelves, and I've noted some of the call numbers." Edna searched her pockets, then recalled putting the slip of paper into her purse. In the secret compartment.

Edwina Gluck took the list and stared at it over her glasses. She looked from it to Edna, back and forth.

"We shall do what we can. Thank you, Mrs. Leddy, for your vigilance." Ms. Gluck scanned the area as if there were a huge waiting line necessitating her frugal expenditure of time.

Edna left the circulation desk taking minor consolation in the fact that she had not enlisted Ms. Gluck's aid in the more serious crime perpetrated by that baggy-trousered fellow. It was enough for Edna to have full recognition that Ms. Gluck had already crumpled the list and tossed it in the trash. She could not know, however, that although Ms. Gluck was innocent of the fact, she was happy to accept the consequences of Herman's gifts: a more stable general circulation tally.

"BASIL, WHATEVER ARE YOU doing under the catalogs?" Hortense asked rhetorically. "They have maintenance people to sweep the dust balls. Do stand up or you'll be mistaken for another murdered body.''

Ms. Gluck, having rid herself of one old lady problem, darted an alarmed look at another who was talking to the floor beneath the card catalogs.

Basil got up, brushed off his pants, and waved his spectacles at his wife.

"Have the police arrived?''

"They have removed the auditor fellow to what I assume to be a more appropriate location, but we're to regroup, minus Mr. Boehm, for questioning.''

Hortense led Basil to Sara Tewksbury's office, Giles Moraise wanting less to do with bodies than with thefts, but the whole questioning session struck them as perfunctory at best, lackadaisical at worst. Unlike their cinematic versions, these officers scattered no powder to reveal telltale fingerprints, used no magnifying glass, inked no one's fingers, took no mug shots. They didn't even collect suspicious-looking particles in glass tubes. They just took a few photos of Leon and whisked him out the back exit in less than an hour.

Even Basil, inured by his profession to the hideous regicides and casual slaughters history is heir to, even he was surprised at the quick dispatch of the matter.

"Quite uncivil of them not to give us a clue about the death; after all, we did sit with the wretched fellow. Got to know something of his modus operandi in the process. There's no doubt his assistant will have a rough time of it, what with the third-quarter tallies being in such straits. Everything's down, from rare books to—to—what was it, dear?''

"Swivel chairs. Down seventeen last year and fourteen this. Can you imagine?" Hortense queried, her amazement renewed.

Though Sara spared little concern for swivel chairs, the bibliographic losses loomed paramount in her mind. Her repeated bids for hastening computerization were in large measure for reasons of security, and were met with cool indifference, or, in the case of Giles Moraise, with open hostility. God knew what the final tallies would reveal this summer.

Meanwhile, she wondered, where in hell was Herman Lobel?

FIVE

HERMAN LOBEL'S DECISION, after depositing the last of his gifts in the Smedley, was to keep a low profile for the rest of the week and fine-tune his existential purpose. When Sara Tewksbury phoned him at home that Thursday morning, he expressed his regrets about the demise of his boss Leon Boehm.

"Did he ask about the cause of death?" Hortense Killingsley interrogated the assistant director as soon as the Smedley doors opened to the public. She and Basil planned to make a full day of it.

"No. He and Leon tended to keep clear of each other. Actually Leon, well, he didn't give his assistant a too heavily shod foot in the audits door. As far as I can see, Herman's knowledge of Smedley procedures is so minimal as to constitute ignorance."

Basil doubled his chin in his shirt collar and squinted. "Why ever was the fellow hired?"

Sara threw up her bangled arms in perplexity. "Take your choice," she enumerated on her several bejeweled fingers: "one, to lend status; two, to bring coffee and doughnuts; three, to be a fall guy; four—"

"Yes, yes, I see," Basil waved her off, recognizing a way of the world he preferred not to.

"In any event," Sara went on, "the autopsy report came in and the results read that Leon Boehm was strangled."

"With a computer cable?" Hortense asked wide-eyed, eager to tackle the devious and insidious.

"The report Giles received," Sara recalled, "didn't specifically mention it—"

"Then it's not ruled out. See there, Basil," Hortense said, pleased that her rush to the violent had been borne out.

"Yes, dear. Are you prepared to enlighten us with a motive—if not the perpetrator—for the crime?"

"Several. First, that letter of evaluation—you remember, under Mr. Boehm's body? A rather nasty critique on Mr. Moraise's part," she confided to Sara.

"Oh, that," Sara acknowledged casually. "Giles's annual evaluations are legendary for their invective. He's got a talent for diatribe, but no one takes him seriously, least of all the board of directors."

"Oh," Hortense said, somewhat disappointed. "Well, number two: discrepant accounts." She was pleased at her resources.

"Any ones in particular? Swivel chairs? Lighting fixtures?" Basil teased.

"Lighting fixtures are holding their own. Swivel chairs . . . there's something amiss there, though I'm more prepared to accept random pilfering—you know, the sort of borrowing undergraduates do with lounge furniture—than genuine conspiracy. There's so little cooperation these days, even in the underworld."

"If you're really into motives," Sara continued, "I'm afraid you'll have to dismiss most, if not all, of the bibliographic accounts. Many sections are reporting tallies up, which is a bit surprising since the last quarter count was way down. We've all been waiting for this thorough count, and so far so good."

"But see there," Hortense raised her index finger and wrinkled her brow, "you're surprised at stability, as well you should be. Books don't just disappear and reappear of their own volition."

"Dear," Basil urged, "I'm certain Dr. Tewksbury has other tasks than to grapple with your profundities—like running a library. And we are here to take advantage of her labors. Our legitimate research is scholarly, not criminal."

"Basil, I merely suggest that no hypothesis ought to be discarded without examination. Even the normal should be regarded with suspicion."

"It is, dear."

Hortense took her husband's meaning and moved out to rare books where she hoped to carry on normally and possibly extend the Indo-European linguistic umbrella with wider application of Grimm's Law. This morning she was in hot pursuit of B drifting to P and D to T after the Great Vowel Shift. On her husband's suggestion, she had gone to a third quarto edition of *The cronicle history of Henry the fift, with his battell fought at Agin Court in France*... and was scanning it for its rendering of Fluellen's Welsh dialect. She was lip-reading a number of alternative pronunciations as well as collating the quarto with a modern Kittredge edition. As she thought she was alone, except for Cyril Prout who had become quite inured to Hortense's verbal foragings, she threw herself into articulating Fluellen's register of discourse in fully audible tones, trying first one inflectional pattern and then another.

"'*Kill* the poys and the luggage? ...'Tis as arrant a piece of knavery, mark you now, as can be offert.'

"'Kill the *poys*...?' Mmm. Well, 'Fortune is painted *plind*...'"

Barney Dibbs, janitoring on the other side of the archive toward which Hortense had her back, ceased his featherdusting and peered between the shelves.

"'...as can be *of*fert...of*fert*?'

"No, no, that's not it," she muttered to herself. "Dad's Boston *a* is screaming through the vowels and Fluellen certainly didn't have a Boston *a*."

"He neverra wuda' hae that," Barney agreed, making light of his interruption. Hortense darted a birdlike look at the janitor through the shelves. His phonological regionalism had never registered with Hortense until this moment.

"Celtic. North Anglesey," she fairly accused him.

"Nae sae farr fra, though I werra a wee ane when we teuk oursels ta—"

"Conway!"

"Llandudno. Sae, ye ken an meikle 'bout me tongue. Folks sae I hae ane ferlie air mysel. E'en dinna bit o' theater wi' the locals. Maist o' Shakespeare."

While most patrons of the Smedley—particularly those deemed worthy of rare book privileges—might have dismissed the dramatic abilities of a janitor, Hortense harbored no preconceptions. Within moments she had established that Barney Dibbs was a true amateur, a lover of the Bard, who both knew whole scenes by heart, and, as he too modestly suggested, had a superb ear for dialect.

As it was silly for them to converse between and above the shelves, Hortense came around to Barney's side of the stack and pushed the third quarto at him.

"Here, you read this like Fluellen would!"

Barney Dibbs silently skimmed the edition for a moment and then began to read it aloud. Hortense's critical ear was perked. The ring of phonetic truth was there.

"Yes, yes, that's it. Modern editors do so bastardize his speech. All this wretched standardization in the name of accessibility. Posh and nonsense! I'm sure *you* know *Shakespeare* knew very well what he was about." Hortense gave Barney an inclusive nod. "He wrote as *people* spoke: substituting p's for b's, t's for d's, whatever. The man had an ear for dialect—of course, I needn't tell you!" She took back the book for further examination.

"Hmm. This quarto here, the third..." Hortense flipped to the colophon. "Oh, sixteen nineteen. I was hoping for sixteen hundred. Besides, if my dim literary background serves me, the sixteen nineteen should read sixteen o eight—though in fact it was not published until sixteen nineteen. Of course, I'm no expert in these matters, hmm..." Hortense put her nose to the volume and took a good sniff. "Chamomile."

"Tay? Ye ken whatna?"

"Yes. Chamomile quite definitely."

Barney poised his duster and shook his head. He took the book and examined it delicately. "Ah, nu sae herre: tha wee bit o' wud in the paper."

Hortense peered quizzically. The import of wood chip slowly dawned on her. "Nineteenth century?" she asked affirmatively.

"A ferlie thing. The uncos a' Glasgow werra wi' the mills. Thai be a-telling me as a wee ane 'o the maikin' o' paper."

"Sulphite bleaching. A rather late development on the paper scene."

"Ye ken sae. Thaer werra time when ony rag werra used—"

"Prohibitively expensive. But you're quite on target, Barney. This sixteen nineteen is not sixteen nineteen any more than I am."

Barney nodded and resumed scanning his beloved author.

Cyril Prout, who had been studiously reading auction catalogs at his desk on the other side of the room, became increasingly curious as to what possible mutual interests Hortense Killingsley and Barney Dibbs might have. Theirs was more than casual conversation. He rose and moved toward the odd couple as if to offer assistance.

Barney was getting into a Gaelic lilt while Hortense was jotting down a phonetic transcription of the janitor's reading. Once he got wound up, he could switch registers, accents, and tempos without the least hesitation. Shut your eyes, Hortense thought, and you might hear an Orson Welles before you. But of course she couldn't shut her eyes as she was hastily transcribing as much of Barney's verbal mimicry as she could.

When Cyril Prout drew up to the two of them, he wasn't sure what to think. That the janitor should be reading Shakespeare—never mind how convincingly—was odd, but no odder than that Professor Killingsley herself should be bobbing up and down from lip to pad, scribbling in strange phonetic ligatures.

"Ahem," Cyril asserted.

Barney lowered the quarto edition and smiled
sheepishly. Hortense stared with a touch of indignation.

"Yes? Can we help you?" she asked.

Cyril was thrown off balance. "I was wondering if
I might be of assistance. You looked—or so it
seemed—as if you needed help."

"With what?" Hortense asked sharply, and then
softened her tone. "Oh, Barney and I here were just
checking on the apparent fact of the operability of
Grimm's Law in Shakespeare's day. There are those
who believe that its influence ended well before the
Empire—the Roman Empire, that is—but evidently
those narrow minds failed to consider its resuscitation in consequence of the Great Vowel Shift."

Cyril Prout was speechless. Barney was smiling.

"I see." Cyril finally excused himself and looked
about for books to straighten.

"Oh, Dr. Prout, while you're here . . . Barney and I
were wondering about this quarto edition. Neither of
us is a bibliographic expert, but it struck us that this
edition has something incongruous about it. The edition date reads sixteen nineteen, but that's preposterous because, as Mr. Dibbs discovered, there are wood
chips in the paper—clear indication of its modernity.
And if that's the case, it shouldn't be in rare books.
See here, a speck. Wood pulp. Are you with me?"

"Hum? Yes, yes. Sulphite bleaching, I see. Eighteen eighties to pinpoint the matter."

Cyril handled the edition carefully at first, and then
with increasing roughness, as if the volume had turned
into a smelly fish. "Where did you find this?" he demanded in alarm.

Hortense and Barney indicated the location across the bookshelf, the place from which X822.33/W3/1619 came.

Prout took the volume and marched around the archive to its shelf space, expecting to find the real third quarto right there. He did not.

"That's odd." It was a word Cyril found himself employing with increasing frequency since joining the Smedley staff. He checked the spine and its number fit right into the shelf sequence. He made rapid mental inventory: had he taken the real third quarto home for safe-keeping?

His mind scanned his not altogether kosher plan. Since his arrival in January, he had been conducting a slow, meticulous search that thus far revealed several missing treasures: the *Eneydos*, Hilton's *Scala Perfecconis*, and the Davies *Sovereigne salve* being only some of the better known, and then there were (according to third-quarter tallies) nineteen others gone (now twenty, though number twenty—the Higden—was identified), nineteen missing and for the most part of unknown import: only the Boehmish mechanistic number remained.

The ignominy of it all forced Cyril to safeguard the honor of the bibliographic world by appropriating ten, perhaps twelve, rare texts in his modest apartment. He was most assuredly not filching, merely securing some of his favorites until such time that the source of the losses was located and plugged.

Even though his home collection was growing out of hand (he simply had to stop), he didn't think he had any Shakespeare. In any event, he certainly wasn't into the vulgar practice of substituting what appeared to be a wretched forgery for rare treasure.

The next several minutes were spent with Cyril scurrying for the shelf card, Barney wondering if it would be appropriate to resume dusting, and Hortense babbling on about her bibliographic ignorance.

"Ah. You're right, Mrs. Killingsley. This—this copy is of a third quarto printed by W. Jaggard, but our real third quarto is sixteen hundred and printed by Thomas Creede, so that *this* book is a doctored copy of a lesser original!" He was holding the volume as if the covers concealed offal. Another treasure gone!

With his packet of shelf cards in hand, Cyril pulled volumes adjacent to the Shakespeare. Their numbers correlated, as did their Renaissance titles—one a Marlowe *Tamberlaine* and the other a Jonson *Volpone*. He pulled out the Marlowe and opened it to the title page. There he found:

Songs and Sonnets Written by the Right Honourable Lord Henry Haward Late Earl of Surrey and Other Published by Richard Tottel June 5, 1557 (Reprint by T. Y. Crownell and Co, Ltd. 1890)

The shelf card and the book spine correlated, but the title page and actual content had no connection to them. Indeed, as Cyril flipped pages, he realized what he held was a cheap nineteenth-century edition of Tottel's famous *Miscellany*. Cyril Prout's deep-set eyes bulged.

"There's—there's some mistake!"

Hortense peered into the volume. "Oh. However did Tottel get between Marlowe's covers?"

Quickly Cyril grabbed *Volpone*, opened it, and found another crummy copy of Tottel's *Miscellany*. "Oh, my God!" He fell back to the shelves for support.

Hortense again looked and tsked. "The *Miscellany* isn't all that bad, though why the Smedley would purchase two—oh, I see..."

Cyril Prout began pulling out volumes randomly, as if in the grip of some nightmare wherein all literary richness had been reduced to Tottel's *Miscellany*. Had some horrible third dimension invaded the Smedley? His own brain? No, no, clearly Hortense Killingsley was seeing Tottel, too.

And so was Barney Dibbs. Though most of the volumes the three of them hauled from their spots were legitimate, Barney found two more Tottels in the next archive, neither of which was so labeled. He frankly admitted not caring for Renaissance ditties. Hortense defended some of the inclusions, especially those by Surrey. "'Thou farest as fruit that with the frost is taken—'" she caroled. Her recitation was interrupted by the sudden concordance of Basil.

"'Today ready ripe, tomorrow all to-shaken,'" he chimed, not without a certain pride in his memory.

"Odd you should quote Surrey, dear, as I've had rather peculiar experiences with him and his companions in Tottel's on the whole redundant collection."

Barney nodded in critical agreement.

Cyril was alternating a strange gaze between the Tottels in hand and the Killingsleys.

"Come, now, my man," Basil assured him, "they're not *so* dreadful. Certainly the collection carried influence disproportionate to its literary worth, but still it's of considerable historical—"

"Dear—"

"—import. Although I must say, the Smedley has gone a bit overboard in Tottel purchasing, hasn't it?" Basil continued in good humor. "Why, dear, you recall that foolish confusion of Tottel among the Carolingians? I did mean to report it... And then," Basil's eyes lit up to full voltage, "there was this clumsy pimply youth who had what turned out to be an armload of Tottels! Remember, dear, last night while you were pulping the potatoes, I told you about that old lady trailing him...?"

Hortense's mouth was agape. Basil gently chucked his wife's chin, urging her mouth into verbalization. She explained what she knew of Tottel's proliferation in rare books.

Turning with an authorial air, Basil announced to the melancholic Prout, "Obviously he's paid you a visit!"

While Basil's statement was not on par with clarifying the nature of quarks or indisputably verifying the parallax theory of the universe, Cyril Prout got the message.

"Oh, my God," he moaned, and again reached for the support of the shelves.

Barney Dibbs quietly picked up his feather duster and continued dabbing books and shelves where he had left off, hoping he wouldn't knock over a Tottel. Basil, too, resumed normalcy by making what inquiry it was that brought him to rare books, and Hortense stood about wondering if "Thou farest as fruit that with the frost is taken" was an example of alliterative survival or revival.

Only the rare books curator was passing up the opportunity for normalcy.

SIX

CYRIL PROUT'S EDENIC WORLD was turning to ashes and dust, or more precisely, to *Miscellanies*, voids, and chintzy copies. What was so various, so beautiful, and so new six months ago, now had neither the *Eneydos*, the Davies, Higden, Shakespeare, nor who knew what else. Now even the irrepressible Killingsleys comported themselves in hushed tones as they darted about rare book archives. And so, too, Edna Leddy (who this day chose to forage in the same area) felt an unusual heaviness in the room. Normally she was a cushion of silence amid the library hum; today she curtailed her breathing and walked on tiptoe so as not to disturb the comatose curator.

Only Sara Tewksbury and Cecil Blinn had no sense of environment as their imposing figures fairly burst into the funereal scene. They stiffened as echoes of their light chatter bounced off the walls and ricocheted in their faces. Basil Killingsley, up to his nose in musty feudal matters, darted an unintentionally piercing scowl in their direction. Sara jolted at its impact, noted the different drummer to which the others drooped, and in particular, noted Cyril Prout slumping over a pile of assortedly numbered books on his desk. She hushed Ceese and approached the morose curator quietly, lightly touching him on the shoulder.

"Cyril?"

"Hum? Oh, yes. Sorry. I, um..." He straightened himself as well as the pile of Tottels. "Ah, Mr. Blinn, nice to see you," he said with failed enthusiasm.

Sara smiled and waved at Basil Killingsley, who reciprocated the gesture in his more usual gentlemanly manner. He then continued his intense fact-finding mission.

In full-barreled tones, Ceese explained that, having checked into Smedley needs with the aid of Sara, he had made a decision on the nature of his donation.

"O' course I haven't looked over the whole operation, but by gum, I'm real set on keepin' hold of them old incunabula," he said with pride.

Basil's alert ear perked at Ceese's resounding words. He marched over to Cyril's desk.

"Yup. Mizz Sara and I were havin' dinner and she was sayin' how fine the rare books stuff is and how it was top-grade. I like that. Just like the wine we were drinkin'. Fine old stuff. Some things just get better with age, ain't that so?" Ceese cheerily nudged Cyril's shoulder.

Cyril's dour countenance brightened. "Oh, I say, that's true. Oldies but goodies. Withstood the test of time," he babbled on in a surge of childlike glee. "And just when rare books is in such need. What with the missing medieval works, and now, well, now *this*!" He waved his hand at the Tottel pile, which brought his ebullience down a peg or two. "The Killingsleys—ah, here's the professor now," Cyril noted. "I was just telling Mr. Blinn—"

"Ceese to my friends."

"Yes, of course, Ceese, that your wife—oh there she is—" Cyril raised his head to indicate the direction from which Hortense's intent mumbling came, "yes, well, that she and I, actually she and our janitor, Barney Dibbs, well, we happened to come upon these cheap modern editions of that Renaissance bestseller scattered through these shelves! Variously numbered and titled on the spines, but look here—" One by one Cyril carelessly flipped open covers to reveal substantially the same title page. "And we found these just by random selection. I can't bear to think of how many more are out there occupying space reserved for treasures. Why, they're virtually metastasizing in rare books! And we've uncovered a Shakespeare third quarto that is no such thing!" Cyril elliptically had returned to the throes of his miscellaneous despair.

Sara looked over Basil's shoulders as he opened several of the editions to confirm the source of Cyril's miserable state. Seeing the *Miscellany* title pages provided her with full report. The Shakespeare 1619 with wood pulp paper was more disturbing, for there was recognizable criminal intent in the tea-stained pages. However, not wishing to advertise the felony (a real third quarto's theft was well beyond misdemeanorial limits), she quietly took up the volume while directing Cyril's attention to the happier issue at hand.

"Cyril, I'm sure Mr. Blinn—Ceese—is anxious to know how he might contribute..."

"Of course. Yes indeed. Certainly."

Cyril summoned himself to search for the latest auction catalogs. As he was doing so, Sara drifted over to where she spied Edna Leddy lurking in tenacious absorption of the PQ 700s spines. With her sixth sense Edna knew she'd been spotted. She slid farther into the archive. Sara went over.

"Hello, Mrs. Leddy. Finding anything good to read?"

Edna was still operating under her delusion that if she didn't look at others, they wouldn't look at her, but the ploy wasn't working. She clasped her gloved hands and smiled old-lady fashion. Sara did not, however, disappear or even appear satisfied with the smarmy smile. Edna found it necessary to reach into the Leddy innards for a source of verbal courage.

"Ms. Tewksbury, is it? I believe I have something to report," she whispered hastily, shutting her thin-veined eyelids and taking a deep breath.

Sara wondered if Edna Leddy was becoming dizzy from sartorial sensitivity. Her tiger-striped jersey and jungle beads were clearly out of sync with lace gloves and lavender scent.

"Yes, I do," she reiterated bravely, fixating on Sara's yellow bone necklace.

"Yes?" Sara urged.

By fits, starts, and then smooth direction, Edna Leddy explained her adventures in the reading room trailing the pudgy intruder and checking out his additions.

"And Ms. Tewksbury, I very carefully copied down the call numbers because—do you know?—all the books the sneaky fellow was putting on shelves, *all* were the same book—the same work, I should say."

Sara's interest in the tale peaked.

"And I just accidentally overheard Mr. Prout say how he found the very same work scattered in his shelves. Now that *is* strange, isn't it?" she asked with a twinkle of excitement in her eye.

"You copied down the call numbers . . . ?"

"Oh, yes. I'm very sorry to say that I reported all this to Ms. Gluck at the circulation desk and I gave her the numbers. Do you know what she did?" Edna asked with a degree of indignation. "Why, she quite coolly thanked me and I could hear her crumple up my notepaper under the desk. I'm not deaf, you know!"

While Sara and Edna were thus engaged over unaccountable additions, Cyril, Ceese, and Basil were eyeing lists of very accountable, notable editions.

"Many fine items here. A splendid array of choice. See here." Cyril's finger went down the list. "Here's an *Eneydos*, and the bottom price isn't bad."

Basil bent to look. "Oh, indeed. Quite reasonable, especially as it never made it to a second edition. A classic instance of Caxton's enthusiasm for—oh, sorry. Please continue."

"Naturally we can't say what it will bring at auction, but," Cyril reread the fine-print description, "if it's as good as it says, it's worth twice, even three times that." Cyril looked up, pleased at the vision of replacing a missing Smedley volume, but within seconds his beam lowered its wattage and his face darkened in wrinkled concern. He grabbed up the auction catalog and pored over the Caxton *Eneydos* description, then lurched to the Hilton *Scala Perfecconis* announcement, then fairly croaked at the sight of Davies's *Sovereigne salve to cure the worlds madness*, 1625. "Oh, my God ... No. Yes. Oh, my God, it *is*!"

Sara, who was clucking dismay at Edna's story, wasn't deaf, either. She silenced herself and Edna, and hastened around the archive to see Cyril uprooting his few tonsured hairs and looking torn, quite torn be-

tween laughter and tears. Basil patiently allowed the
man his fit, while Ceese just looked bewildered.

Cyril looked desperately at Sara, clutched the catalog, and spluttered; "They're here. Oh, my God, right
here." He shook the catalog as if "they" might spill
out. "The *Eneydos*, the Hilton, the Davies—oh,
oh—" Cyril clutched his heart. "Higden—wait, wait.
Yes. Our fourteen ninety-five Wynkyn de Worde: G.
van Os initials and all!"

Basil grabbed the catalog and fairly ate up the description with his eyes.

"The Smedley copies? Are you sure?" Sara asked.

"Absolutely. Positively. There's no doubt. *This* is
the edition I handled in this library. It's got to be."

Hortense, hearing her husband's adamant asser-
tions, left off her muffled articulations and joined
what was now a mob at Cyril's desk.

"Does it?" she asked, nodding to the others.

"See for yourself," Basil challenged, thrusting the
auction catalog under his wife's eyes.

"Mmm. It's a shame that Higden cut short his history at thirteen twenty-seven, wasn't it, dear? He never
got to the Hundred Years War, though he himself
lived another—what was it?—thirty-seven years?"

"Ah, yes," Basil considered seriously. "Of course
we do have to allow for his early start, *ab ovo*, as they
say," he chuckled, largely at the prospect of again
seeing the volume.

"The Lord's creation, I believe," Hortense corrected, "was pre-*ovo* . . . ovum?"

Basil gave her a sideways glance. "Ablative: *ovo*."

The rest of the cluster around Cyril's desk did not
decline.

As Cyril was marshaling his spirits, Giles Moraise
was marshaling his wits. He had just that morning
concluded the deal on the Americana editions he'd
been lusting after, and within the week the medieval
works would be auctioned and the cash transferred.
Oh frabjous day! he frivolously thought as he settled
in to more legitimate tasks, like composing the re-
mainder of his annual evaluations of his staff. Despite the circumstantially incriminating evaluation
found by Leon Boehm's body, Giles had no intention
of tempering his judgments. In fact, he found his
giddy spirits sharpening his verbal barbs against his
underlings. He was savoring past instances of their
opposition or folly for which he could now retaliate.
He recalled Edwina Gluck's intolerance of patrons
and her snippiness over tallies; Winifred Sisson's high-
pitched squeals and tendency to panic... "Oh ho,
callou callay," Giles merrily sang. Sara Tewksbury's
evaluation would be his gem: "emotionally untidy;
conducts self with insolence bordering on the criminal; vulgar dress habits suitable for tribal rituals or
Caligulan orgies." He chortled over his delicious
phrasing and sweet revenge. "Rating: zero."

So it was that when the three rare book aficionados
foaming with quizzical chatter burst into the director's sanctuary, Giles's private glee was forced inward
and required some fancy lip pursing to keep it in. As
the usually dyspeptic curator was evidencing an un-
seemly degree of enthusiasm, Giles strove, by personal example, to curb such unprofessional behavior.
He sat bolt upright, swiftly organized the papers on his
desk, and then, and only then, did he heed the bub-
bling entrants.

Cyril Prout took one look at his boss and recognized the need to exercise some sort of negative capability. He had sufficient grasp on himself to calculate his presentation: the good news first, then (alas) the bad. Unfortunately, he had no way of knowing that the good news would not be read as such by Giles. That rare books had a stable tally for the first time in months was not comforting, as Giles himself had been filching items; that the rich Texan was settling upon the purchase of incunabula was more than discomforting: it was infuriating.

"What?" Giles exploded, blowing his cool smack in the wealthy benefactor's face. "It's ridiculous—absurd in this day and age. The Smedley can't possibly keep up with the Huntingtons, Folgers, or Pierpont Morgans." He was nearly screeching as he rose, flinging his expensive swivel chair against the wall. Basil made a mental note to report the carelessness to Hortense who'd factor such rough treatment into her burgeoning theory of accountability. "The British market's untouchable, overpriced. The dollar's unstable, the European climate is—is—why, why, it's anti-American!" Giles's eyes, not to say his whole corporeal being, were expanding to dangerous purple proportions. Basil's thoughts shifted along paramedical lines.

"Now, Mr. Moraise," he spoke as if to a flunking student, "Mr. Blinn here has the best of intentions, I'm quite sure—"

"Damn intentions! Idiotic! Why—why—" Giles raced toward Cecil Blinn hoping to bring him to his senses.

"Look, Ceese old bean," he said, flinging his arm around the Texan's large back, "you must see the brilliant opportunities in Americana. The market hasn't been this rich in years. Americana for Americans, you know. No, no, we cannot throw money away to the foreigners and throw ourselves off course."

Cyril wrinkled his brow. He was unaware of any course the Smedley had.

Giles's shirt back was sopping with nervous perspiration and his cranium was throbbing with thoughts of his threatened Americana empire. He had to move fast. He had a solid base—or would have by the end of the month when the bills were due, but there were other rare editions to scan, purchases to be made, bargains to be struck. He had to salvage his Americana wing: yes, the Giles Moraise American Wing of the Smedley Library. Or maybe—years from now, of course, but certainly not to be facetiously dismissed—the Giles Moraise Library of Americana. There was pleasing assonance to the name.

Meanwhile, however, to relax his teeming brain, Giles was mentally composing a particularly lacerating evaluation of Cyril Prout, should that—that plebeian Texan be allowed to carry out his witless project. He made a few visual notes on the ceiling: lacks assertion, vision; inability to formulate long-range goals decisively...

Cyril was so desolate over his director's apoplectic reception of the good news that he wisely denied him the bad: the discovery of a cheap copy of Shakespeare, the sudden and inexplicable appearance of Tottels everywhere, and the equally sudden and inexplicable appearance of missing Smedley medi-

evaliana in auction catalogs. Cyril's refuge in sad
contemplation of Giles's desk edge, as well as a fresh
failure at composure on his boss's part, were interrupted by the sudden and unannounced entrance of
Herman Lobel.

"Yes, can we help you?" Neither Giles nor Cyril
recognized Herman as a staff person.

"Oh, hi. Yeah," he began inauspiciously, looking
around for a cushy seat and banging his scrolled magazine against his knee.

Giles's beady eyes radiated contempt for the tubby,
unkempt creature, whereas Cyril saw the intrusion as
opportunity for retreat. He mumbled professional excuses and turned to Basil and Ceese. Basil nodded in
recognition of the sloppy entrant's total disregard as
characteristic of today's youth. Without a word, he
rose and shepherded his fellow travelers out the door.

Herman watched them exit. "Yeah, well, I'm here
about a raise..."

SEVEN

WHAT WITH VOLUMES proliferating and solutions nowhere in sight, Edna Leddy traded in her passive role as silent browser for one of bibliographic activism. With what she read as encouragement from Dr. Tewksbury over her discovery of the Tottel additions, and despite Ms. Gluck's manifest indifference, Edna more or less considered herself chief undercover agent for all library materials. No longer did she spend her days at the Smedley as her mood dictated; now she had a mission, a service to perform. No longer were the idle browser's gloves and trim little hat appropriate attire; now she was getting down to business: to handling, examining, and scrutinizing suspicious library material, however dusty and germ-ridden it might be.

In reference, as Edna shuffled through the bound editions of *The Journal of Waste and Sewage Disposal*, pulling each volume off the shelf, hastily flipping its pages and stuffing it back in its slot, Miss Sisson thought Edna's behavior odd, but as the journal was not a source of great interest (a gift in perpetuity from an overzealous environmentalist), she felt the rare attention would at least clear the cobwebs.

In the reading room, her scurrying and fussing on shelves and jotting in her paisley notebook did not go unnoticed either. In his corner wing chair M. Farb crinkled his *Le Monde* and from above its Gothic masthead observed Edna's altered demeanor. He also noticed the now familiar figure of the portly professor who was, *merci à Dieu*, behaving regularly, and nodded in his direction. The professor rose and approached the distinguished Frenchman.

"How do you do? Basil Killingsley here. Medieval English history. The Hundred Years War and all that..."

"Ah, oui," the Frenchman responded, standing and bowing slightly. "Michel Farb, at your service."

"Ahem," Basil continued, feeling a bit silly now that he'd followed his ill-defined impulse. "Well, I know you're chairman of the board and all that, and, um, I'm not sure if anyone's told you of the wretched Tottel business?"

"Pardonnez, was he in the war?"

"Hmm? Oh, the Hundred Years—no, no. That woman there," Basil indicated with a raise of his brow to avoid the rudeness of pointing, "that's Edna Leddy. She's coming up with Tottels—Tottel's *Miscellany*, a rather overrated verse anthology from the English Renaissance—all over the place." The professor had the good sense to recognize his own dithering, but as M. Farb had, quite on his own, the intention of pursuing Mme Leddy, he needed little encouragement. He bowed and waved Basil to lead the way.

"Pardonnez, madame," M. Farb graciously began so as not to startle the preoccupied prim lady.

"Oh." Edna Leddy started, blushing at being so suavely addressed.

"Forgive me, but I am a very curious man. Allow me to introduce myself: Michel Farb, at your service." He made a small bow and clicked his heels. "And this is Professor Killingsley."

"Oh," Edna reiterated, flustered at not having a free hand to be given over to M. Farb's gesture. "Um, ah, Edna Leddy here, how do you do?" She clutched a volume of Joseph Conrad and extended her fingertips.

"*Certainement,* it is not my affair, but as we are—how does one say?—of the same party...?"

Edna blushed, not fully sure of the party to which they all belonged.

"The Tottels, you know," Basil added from the rear, seeing Edna's confusion.

"Oh. Oh, yes. My goodness, you know about them?" Given such unexpected recognition, Edna's old Leddy reserves burbled to the surface. "Forty-six to date, forty-six silly Tottels, and I just found number forty-six right here in place of—what is it?—yes, Joseph Conrad's *Heart of Darkness.* See here," she showed M. Farb, pleased that he was genuinely interested.

"*Mais oui,* this is not right, no, *pas de tout.*" He pored over the page, flipped to the text (genuine *Miscellany*), and was evidently more alarmed than Edna had any hope of expecting. "And you say this does not alarm the librarians, all the same works?"

"Oh, Dr. Tewksbury's very alarmed; it's just that Ms. Gluck—you know, the sour woman who sits at the circulation desk?" Basil nodded sympathetically. "I'm collecting as many of the call numbers as I can for Dr. Tewksbury, and you can be sure I won't give a one to Ms. Gluck."

Michel smiled at Edna's umbrage and winked at the professor. As Basil's thirty-five years among undergraduates had provided him with a keen sense of incipient amatory interests, he did what he often did when wishing to abscond gracefully: he checked his watch.

"Oh, dear. It's Friday, nearly five, and funeral time."

INDEED, WHILE MICHEL and Edna were getting better acquainted, a slim showing of the Smedley staff was bidding its farewell to Leon Boehm's remains at Parkwell Cemetery. The funeral was a dreary affair, made more so by the sparse attendance. As auditor, and therefore watchdog on spending and accountability, Leon didn't have many collegial friends; as megalomaniac loner, he didn't want many friends; as single offspring and bachelor, he didn't have many relatives. The one aunt who could be located had to be prodded into recollection of her nephew's existence, and even at that did not think his funeral sufficient grounds for a trip east from Utah. The Smedley contingent attended the last rites out of a variety of unsentimental motivations. Obligation as his boss brought Giles Moraise; something similar, combined with a certain sense of decency, brought Sara Tewksbury; decency, curiosity, a need to pursue loose threads they had stumbled on only two days before in that dingy basement office brought Basil and Hortense Killingsley. And Cecil Blinn, partly as member of the discovery party, partly to trail along with Sara and the Killingsleys, who were growing on him, made up the fifth of the funeral party. Six, if one counted Leon Boehm.

"Odd, isn't it," Hortense remarked after the pastor mumbled minimal encomia over the lowering cas-

ket, "that his assistant—whatshisname?—didn't put
in an appearance."

"Herman Lobel," Sara supplied. "Yes, it is, but he
seems to have been making himself scarce for a long
time. Most of the Smedley staff don't even know Leon
had an assistant."

"Whatever do you mean?" Giles Moraise questioned, as if his own professional reputation were at
stake. "Herman Lobel has been doing a fine job, and
just because *you* don't see him milling around wast-
ing time in chitchat, doesn't mean that *he's* at fault."

Sara was astounded at her boss's regard for the
nonentity, to say nothing of his approval. She had
never before heard him speak well of anyone.

"Are we talking about the same Herman Lobel?
The assistant auditor who knows as much about the
Smedley accounts as—"

"Dr. Tewksbury, it is *you* who are the ignorant
party, both with regard to Smedley auditing and the
person of Herman Lobel. He's a fine young man with
a future. He'll do well for the Smedley."

Sara decided against arguing, but a fishy smell was
assaulting her olfactory nerves.

"I've made him chief auditor," Giles asserted with
haste in an effort to close the topic.

Cecil Blinn smiled and tried to think of something
distracting to say. "Folks ever find out what did in this
poor feller?"

Sara crossed her eyes and rolled them around their
sockets.

"Speaking of odd," Hortense continued as if her
last odd topic, Herman Lobel, hadn't caused enough

trouble, "the police haven't been very efficient in following up—certainly not with us, have they, Basil?"

Basil, about to murmur some mollification, was cut short by his run-on wife. "I mean the man clearly murdered, motives flourishing in all quarters, and our tax dollars paying their salaries—"

"Have you something more to contribute, Mrs. Killingsley?" Giles asked in challenge.

"Well, clearly the audits—the book tallies are approaching hopeless confusion with all those Tottels—"

"With what?" Giles asked in genuine puzzlement.

"Tottels. Tottel's *Miscellany*? They're springing up on every shelf. Surely you've heard? Why, how many was it, Basil, that we—Barney Dibbs and I—came upon randomly in rare books? Close to a dozen as I recall. To say nothing of the evident forgery of Shakespeare's third quarto!"

Giles Moraise was looking pale and panicky, though he exerted himself to maintain normalcy. His clenched jaw, however, was a dead giveaway.

"Oh, my God," Sara moaned, and then noticed the clergyman giving her a slantwise look. "That's right. Cyril was just about weeping over them and Edna Leddy—"

"Who?"

"Edna Leddy—a regular, and far more prominent than Herman Lobel," Sara muttered. "She's sort of appointed herself chief tracker of these strange volumes on the shelves and says they're everywhere."

"They are indeed," Basil confirmed.

The additional details did not make Giles appear any healthier. He was torn between minimizing his ignorance of an issue that was apparently well publicized, blaming Leon Boehm's simplistic tally system (and thereby tastelessly speaking ill of the dead at the gravesite), and admitting that Leon's methods—and now, presumably, Herman's—were inadequate, a line of pursuit that fed Tewksbury's costly bid for sophisticated computerization, which would effectively and immediately eliminate any slush funds into which Giles had been dipping, to say nothing of calling attention to the actual state of Smedley holdings on the whole as well as, more specifically, in rare books.

"Oh, those," he said, striving for a casual tone.

EIGHT

"GOING ONCE, GOING TWICE, sold to the Widener for ten five. Next: Item Seven four eight six, sixteenth century, Venice, Aldine Press. Petrarch Songs and Sonnets, twenty-eight folios, incomplete."

"These folks sure do move along," Ceese noted to his cohorts Cyril Prout and Basil Killingsley. "A feller hardly gets a chance to figure out what's what."

The confluence of Sotheby's rare book offerings and Ceese's cash necessitated an expedition to the Monday auction in downtown Boston. The room was crowded and bristling with professional excitement, but sober in comparison with Cyril Prout's giddy glee. The news of Ceese's incunabula interests, to say nothing of his Texan generosity, had done much to restore Cyril's bibliognostic enthusiasm. He had to temper himself.

"Now take it easy, Ceese. Let's not get careless. A lift of a finger, tilt of the head, why, the mere raise of an eyebrow might make us reluctant purchasers. The incunabula we're interested in should be coming up shortly, but let's not breathe too easily till then."

Cyril Prout was nervous; he hadn't been to all that many auctions himself. At the Smedley, and at his previous assistant curator post, his responsibilities tended to be more maintenance than acquisition. Until recently, the funds simply were not there, especially as the American dollar had been tottering in the foreign markets. Now, however, what with the strength of the dollar, the balance of trade deficits, and a host of other reasons no one really understood, now was the time to buy. And all the better that Cecil Blinn would pay.

Basil was busy scanning the catalog and the updated auction sheet. He wished they'd come earlier, before the bidding started, so he might have gotten a closer look at some of the wares. Not that he doubted the Higden was *the* Higden.

"Sold to the Rockefeller for nine fifty-five." The auctioneer's gavel came down.

"Remember, Ceese," Cyril warned as much for his own benefit, "let me do the bidding, and if I stop, it's because enough is enough. Sometimes a private party wants a particular item so desperately that price is no object, but we have to hang onto a sense of perspective."

"Mmm. Throws the whole market off to overbid," Basil concurred. "To say nothing of the effects on the scholarly world."

What effects the scholarly world might incur did not plague either Ceese or Cyril, as each was absorbed by his own brand of excitement. Cyril was calculating the time and noting the top price for the first item of interest to them: the *Scala Perfecconis*. He longed to touch it, to peruse Hilton's mystical logic in early print. True, it was a 1525 edition and therefore not technically an incunabulum, but it was a Wynkyn de Worde (London, Fletestrete at the sygne of the Sonne) and that rang good to his ears.

Basil pointed to the entry on the sheet. "Probably resurrected as ammunition against Lutherans," he said knowingly. "Truly stupendous the contribution of the printing press to the Protestant cause. But for the invention, Luther might have been simply another heretic consigned to oblivion. Then again we must not neglect the contribution from the plague, unlikely as it is. Need for clean linen, you know. Rag paper and all that."

Ceese and Cyril were all eyes and smiles watching the transactions up in the front of the room.

"Item seven four nine nine, Hilton, Walter: *Scala Perfecconis*. Imprint thirty-one March fifteen twenty-five. London, Fletestrete by Wynkyn de Worde."

The Smedley contingent moved up closer and Cyril signaled on the opening bid. He waited nervously for a counterbid.

"Do I hear one thousand?"

A moment went by, with Cyril pursing his lips in hope of a speedy bargain. Apparently a hand went up in the rear, though neither Cyril nor Basil caught sight of the bidder.

"Eleven hundred, do I hear eleven hundred?"

Cyril raised his index finger.

"Twelve, do I hear twelve?"

Basil turned around and saw the arm dart up and down. The owner of the arm was not visible.

"Thirteen, do I have thirteen?"

Cyril's index finger again made its rise, though more cautiously than before.

"Fourteen, do I have fourteen?"

No one stirred. After another call for fourteen and another pause, item 7499 went once, twice, and was sold to the Smedley for thirteen.

"It's still reasonable," Cyril assured himself and Ceese, "though I'd like to know who our competition was. I hope he doesn't want our other choices."

Within an hour, an *Eneydos* translated by Caxton, a Davies *A New Post: with sovereigne salve to cure the worlds madness*, and the infamous Higden were legally back in the Smedley's possession. The same anonymous hand had made cautious bids on all three, carefully withdrawing when the competition's (i.e., Cyril's) enthusiasm waned. Basil tried to locate the body belonging to the arm, but feared popping up and having his gesture interpreted as a bid on God knew what. Oddly, after the Higden bidding, in which there was heated interest, Basil turned around and saw a familiar, exiting back. To whom did it belong? The jacket was of the same material as the sleeve around the bidding arm (though he couldn't be absolutely positive) and of the same—or similar—material he had recently seen up close. He pondered, but his mind's eye could image only a blank-faced largish male. A beaming Cecil Blinn and an excited Cyril Prout cut short his mental fine-tuning.

"Look, we have them," Cyril crooned, hugging the volumes to his chest.

Ceese was grinning, his large torso puffed out in Texan pride. "Now that weren't a heap to spend. Why, I tell you fellers, I blow lots more in an hour than that—and get a whole lot less."

"Your generosity will not go unnoticed. Indeed, each of these volumes will be attributed as your personal gift."

"They are the missing Smedley editions, I take it?" Basil asked.

"Oh yes, definitely. But there's nothing we can do about it really. I did register the particulars with Sotheby's authorities, and they'll do what checking they can, but any ill-gotten items would have been laundered through several fences, so to speak," Cyril said without much hope.

The three exited into the corridor as the auctioneer was moving to a new lot. Ceese looked back, still fascinated with the operations, and since the afternoon had been such a bargain, gave a passing thought to picking up some extras. Maybe he ought to get a few— what were they auctioning?—early American books? No, he considered, better not; better stick with the real old incunabula. He scanned the room for a last good look, and just as he turned to follow Cyril and Basil, he saw—yes, it was Giles Moraise. Instinctively his hand went up to wave hello, only to find himself acknowledged as the nineteen-hundred-dollar bid. Giles turned to see who dared raise the price of Cotton Mather letters, holographs that they were. He darted around again, hoping he hadn't been seen by the porcine Texan with the puzzled grin on his face. Oh, my God, he thought, crumpling into his seat, not even thinking of the Mather matter.

"Going once, going twice, sold—sold to the gentleman in the rear for nineteen hundred."

Ceese smiled and wondered what he bought.

"WHAT ON EARTH was Giles Moraise doing there?" Hortense exclaimed, as if she held exclusive rights to the director's whereabouts.

"Bidding, dear," Basil replied calmly, filling in for Ceese, who'd paused in his tale.

"I sure hope the Smedley has a likin' for—what in heck? What's this here feller Cotton Mather?" Ceese laughed at his own expense.

"Mr. Moraise apparently thought so," Basil assured him.

"But he had no authorization," Sara Tewksbury said with mild indignation. "And don't tell me that he was making a personal purchase." As she spoke her eye gleaned the pudgy figure of Herman Lobel exiting the reference room.

"What's odd is that he didn't say hello to you," Hortense noted, pleased to be sniffing a whiff of strangeness.

"Who? Oh, Giles isn't big on social amenities," Sara responded, "though I'd have thought curiosity—or professional concern—would have overridden his customary rudeness. After all, you were there buying for 'his' library, and God knows we can use the additions."

"But not," Hortense winked slyly, "of Tottel!"

As the infamous name was uttered, Edna Leddy came by with what she assumed was a Miss Marple investigatory smile on her prim lips. Close on her left was the debonair figure of Michel Farb. As the couple crossed the group's path, they nodded with the degree of familiarity each wished to claim. Edna slithered up to Sara and whispered ventriloquist fashion: "Fifty-three between rare books and reference." With a wink and a nod, she and Michel walked on.

Hortense looked at her watch. "Good Lord, it's twenty past four and that man isn't reading *Le Monde*!"

Basil and Ceese looked at Hortense as she offered what she considered an explanation: "Perhaps he's smitten?"

Before, however, embroidery could be stitched on that cloth, and before Ms. Gluck could reach the loitering group with clear notification of their disruption of library protocol, Barney Dibbs came racing down the hall headed straight for the lobby mob.

"Ow, bless me auld mither! Lord hae mercy. Doc Tewksbury, ye mustna be a'comin'. An mickle scaith! An terrible mishanter!"

Barney's Celtic theatrics froze the group.

"A ferlie thing as e'er I sae." He bobbed in recognition of Hortense and the gentlemen. "Ye mustna be a'comin'," he repeated to Sara, who stood rooted in place.

"What is it, Barney? Has our leader met with an early demise? You can tell us since Mr. Blinn and the Killingsleys have already witnessed our seamier side."

"Huh? An ye ken whatna?"

"Ken what?"

"The verra news I hae come ta tell ye."

"What news, Barney?"

"That the auld Clootie haen him by the craigie."

"Clootie?"

"The deil, ma'am. Mr. Moraise, he's dead."

Hortense's wide eyes settled on a wouldn't-you-know look. Sara turned Barney on his heels and gestured him to lead the way. Ms. Gluck, all ears at the circulation desk, became preoccupied with fingering overdue notices as the shocked group shuffled down the hall, murmuring rhetorical questions.

Barney Dibbs had wisely locked Giles Moraise's office, leaving the director as he found him: face-down on the Aubusson carpet behind the leather-tooled desk and (expensive) swivel chair. The bloody gash on the back of his head spoke its tale.

"We can rule out poison, strangulation, and probably heart attack," Hortense concluded swiftly, "but not carelessness. Just look at the mess on this carpet. Did he have a wife?"

"Not for the last half dozen years. They divorced—incompatibility, I'd guess. She's in California and I doubt if she'd think his murder worth the airfare."

Sara was tuning into Hortense's sensational wavelength, and Basil was eyeing all surfaces. Ceese was ogling the body.

"He's still gotta be warm," he noted with questioning authority.

"Assuming you're not the perpetrator," Hortense peered into Ceese's face, "your deduction is based on your identification of Mr. Moraise at the auction...?" She held up her index finger, signaling a moment's delay, bent down, and touched Giles's flesh. "He is warm," she confirmed.

"That is the very fabric, the very cut of the cloth!" Basil exclaimed.

"Basil, this is scarcely the moment for sartorial concerns—"

"That sleeve, along with that cuff link, was raised several times this afternoon at the auction—"

"Yessirree! Now ain't that a kick in the pants?" Ceese shook his head. "And I was sayin' how Mr. Moraise just about dug himself into his seat when he saw me wavin'—my wavin' that bought me them there Cotton Mather letters."

"Well then, unless you and Basil are in cahoots," Hortense tallied, "you have been together since and are therefore exempt from suspicion."

Ceese hadn't been aware that he was suspect, and Basil thanked his wife for clearing their names.

"Dr. Prout, however, is not among us and is thus to be counted among the suspect."

"As are yourself and Dr. Tewksbury here, to say nothing of all persons in and around the Smedley for the last hour." Basil parlayed the list to his wife.

"You're quite right, dear."

Barney Dibbs was the only one to object to being classified among the potential felons.

"I was th' ane that found him. I wouldn'a gone an' told ye if I haen a'kilt him."

Though Hortense was prepared to use her devious logic theory on Barney, she thought better of it and allowed Barney's exemption. In fairness Sara couldn't mind being included, as she had often fantasized as much.

"As I was saying before being cleared of murder by my wife, Mr. Moraise was the person who was bidding against us."

Ceese looked quizzical, but before verbalizing the obvious question, Hortense offered the answer.

"Ah! To jack up the price! Which means that Mr. Moraise is the party responsible for the thefts." She looked around smugly.

Sara pondered a moment and thought out loud: "So Giles stole Smedley books, placed them in auction, bid up the prices and . . . ?"

Basil had drifted back to scrutinizing shelves and carefully opening cabinets and drawers.

"Mmm. Interesting. Perhaps he was upping prices to spend on his own collection. A modest, but I'd say semi-precious, collection of Americana here. A Hawthorne... *Thrice Told Tale*?" Basil looked up and repeated the unfamiliar title.

"Not 'twice?' Or 'tales' in the plural?"

"Thrice; singular number. And here." Basil picked up what looked like a very old notebook. He opened the cover and read, "Call me Ishmael." He flipped the pages. "Perhaps a holograph, an early draft. None of the whaling chapters as far as I can see." He picked up another item and opened it. "Emerson's *Essays*. A first edition, eighteen forty-one."

"So he used the take to buy this here stuff," Ceese noted, taking pleasure in his own deduction.

"Precisely," Basil confirmed, glad to see the group of one mind, however slow some were in arriving there.

THE POLICE TOOK THEIR TIME arriving, bringing the same team that had dealt with Leon Boehm's remains. And the modus operandi was pretty much the same: no fingerprinting, no gathering of telltale clues or any noticeable forensic investigation. Hortense Killingsley could barely contain her heightened sense of civic dudgeon.

"Look, lady," the sergeant in charge whined with hands on his hips.

"Killingsley. Hortense. Doctor, Professor, Ms., Mrs. Whichever you choose."

"Look, lady, we got a million cases like this one. The morgue's spilling over with corpses—must be an epidemic. Suicide, homicide, manslaughter, accident, you name it."

"Sergeant, I needn't point out that getting bashed on the back of one's head can hardly be given out as suicide or accident. We are quite clearly dealing with some degree of murder."

Sergeant Kinney looked at Hortense as if she were of another species. He took a deep breath, nodded to the medical team to remove the body, pulled a notepad from his back pocket, and flipped it open.

"You Hortense Killingsley? And," the sergeant looked around, "that your husband Basil Killingsley? And that," he pointed at Sara, "Sara Terksbury—"

"Tewksbury."

The sergeant shut his eyes and then opened them on Ceese. "You. Who are you? You weren't around for the last body."

Sara rushed in to help. "This is Mr. Cecil Blinn, a generous patron of the Smedley."

Ceese smiled broadly and began to extend his friendly Texan hand. Sensing the sergeant's indifference, he withdrew the offer and decided against a first-name basis.

"And I suppose none of you knows anything about this—this body any more than you did the last one?"

"Sergeant, you can't presume—" Sara broke in, siding with Hortense's sense of taxpayer outrage.

"Lady—pardon me—Mizz Tewksbury. I don't presume to know what you folks do in this library that generates dead bodies, but this place is straining its per capita limit and frankly gives me the creeps. According to my notes from last week, none of you knew anything about—whatshisname—Leon Boehm's death—and, as a matter of fact, two of you didn't even know him, right?''

Hortense looked around as if she'd been insulted and expected her companions in ignorance to rally round.

"Sergeant," Basil spoke sensibly, "are you suggesting that we are of no material use in your investigation and therefore can go about our business?"

"I am."

"But Mr. Moraise was at the auction bidding up—" Hortense insisted as if she had a clear line on the murderer.

"Yes, indeed," Sara jumped in enthusiastically, stirring up her toothy jewelry. "Bidding up a storm for the Smedley. It wasn't a couple of hours ago that he was alive and bidding. I understand he got a few good buys for us—some you might be interested in, Professor Killingsley..." She threw the ball of distracting conversation to Basil, hoping Hortense wouldn't press her knowledge of Smedley shady operations.

"My, yes," Basil agreed heartily, crinkling up his nose in scholarly interest. "I do hope he grabbed up Orosius. A simply marvelous account from creation on—commissioned, they say, by Alfred the Great— the Great Bun Burner, heh, heh. Um, there was a similarly ambitious work by Nennius, but he tends to be overpriced by the Arthurian contingent."

A knock on the office door cut short Basil's reminiscence.

Edna Leddy and Michel Farb were beaming in the doorway looking very much a couple.

"Ms. Gluck said you were in here," Edna said to Sara as if no one else were present. "Michel—Monsieur Farb and I were just..." Edna's eyes caught sight of the others and riveted on Sergeant Kinney's uniform. "Oh, dear. Has something happened? Are the police looking into the Tottel affair?" She tittered and blushed. A distinct waft of Pernod permeated her environs.

"*Pardonnez*. Madame Leddy and I, we—"

"Ah, yes. You've been enlisted to tally the Tottels?" Sara again rushed in with exuberance. "They really do deserve special attention, and Mrs. Leddy here has been an absolute peach in helping us out." She encircled the small lady's shoulders affectionately, pressing her arm bangles slightly.

The unexpected encomium on Edna's modest efforts left her flushed and speechless.

"Meanwhile," Sara went on too buoyantly for the circumstances, "the sergeant here has more important tasks than to listen to a catalog of the Smedley holdings, and so, Sergeant Kinney, if we can be of no further help...?"

"Absolutely none. We'll call you if we need you." He turned and exited, muttering.

As soon as the door shut, Sara collapsed in a heap in Giles's leather swivel chair.

"I'm so sorry. That was terribly foolish of me," Hortense remonstrated with herself. "Unless the police launch a full-scale investigation, there's no need to provide them with ammunition tarnishing our scholarly sanctity."

"Surely the Tottels...?" Edna Leddy meekly trailed off, looking quizzically to Monsieur Farb.

"*C'est vrai.* What Madame Leddy means, as I understand, that is, the many books of Tottels are *pour la plupart* additions and therefore they represent, *entre nous*, a foolish prank. Troublesome, *naturellement*, but nothing more."

Sara looked around at the variously informed persons sharing the common bond of bibliophilia.

"I'm afraid, Mrs. Leddy, Mr. Farb, the police were not here about our Tottel problem. They were here because the Smedley director, Giles Moraise, was—well, I guess, murdered."

"No guessing about it!" Hortense added emphatically. "And let's not inflate the police's custodial role to anything approximating investigation."

Edna and Michel were as bewildered by Hortense's remarks as they were by Sara's.

"Sure's odd about them Tottel books—that somebody'd be adding to the stock while the director here was filching—"

Ceese's genuine dismay smote Edna's sensitivity as much as did the content of his comment. M. Farb was aghast at the accusation.

"*Pardonnez,* but I do not understand. Is Mr. Moraise a thief?"

"Was. He's dead now. Beaned," Hortense added knowingly to Edna, whose shoulders lurched protectively at the word. She swiftly filled the couple in on the latest Smedley demise as if such was a regular occurrence, and then glanced at the clock.

"Oh, goodness, it's well past six and my crockpot will make mush of the mutton if I don't—"

"Mais oui," M. Farb added, shaking free the spate of criminal activity. "Perhaps I may persuade Madame Leddy under the *très triste* circumstances to dine with me this evening?" The suave Frenchman bowed slightly and gallantly offered his arm. It was shyly accepted. Edna gave the group a girlish backward glance as her partner ushered her out.

"Basil," Hortense turned toward her husband, who was poking through texts, "surely you wouldn't begrudge these loyal Smedlians some of our stew? The crock's quite large and I've over five pounds of meat in it. We could microwave a few potatoes and—"

"—and exchange information, thrash about in several detectional directions, and perhaps nab our killer before dessert?" Basil winked at the group.

"Well, I see no harm in pooling perspectives on the strange happenings around here. It's not as if the authorities are exhausting themselves..."

"My wife and I cordially invite you to our house for dinner." Basil bowed formally to Sara and Ceese. "No need to dress, make reservations or excuses. My wife will have it no other way."

Hortense was pleased to see her husband falling in with her spirit.

NINE

"OH, GOOD. THE BRIE'S not too runny. Basil, would you bring those funny-looking crackers when you come?" Hortense Killingsley spoke in various directions.

"You have some home," Sara Tewksbury said for want of words for the decor of scattered magazines, books, papers, and *objets d'art*.

Cecil Blinn agreed, looking about for a place to sit.

"I've no legitimate excuse for the clutter. It's always threatening to collapse the floorboards, and even though we've eleven rooms, neither of us can bring ourselves to throw out a thing. We're always casting about for a space to park. I'm not sure whether the situation's improved or worsened with Xeroxing. There's always more information to keep abreast of and more sophisticated means: print, diskette, cassette, video. The mind's got all it can do to keep track of where it all is." Hortense looked about hopelessly, still holding the cheeseboard. "I'm certain the Malahide Castle couldn't have been in this disarray when—who was it?—stumbled on the Boswell papers—"

"Pottle," Basil responded as he came through the jalousie doors from the kitchen. He held a tray of wineglasses and was looking about for a level spot to place it. "Do you mind shifting that pile," he nodded to Sara, "to...um...over there?" His bushy brows indicated another precariously cluttered table. "The potatoes are in the microwave, salad's in the spinner, and dessert's in the Cuisinart ready for pulping,'' he added triumphantly. "Now if someone—ah, Ceese?''

"Huh? Yessiree.''

"You're a Texan and should know something of drilling. Would you be good enough to uncork the wine? If you'll excuse me a moment, I'll record the evening news so we won't miss out on a dose of reality.''

"Good idea, and if we're pressed for conversation, we can always tune in with dessert.'' Hortense spoke merrily, shoving cheesed crackers at each in turn. "I was joking,'' she added when no one smiled.

Ceese was engrossed by the corkscrew, which he held every which way in hopes its modus operandi might become apparent.

Sara was surveying the piles of books, articles, and magazines of every variety, turning over a leaf here and there and looking puzzled.

"Aha,'' Ceese snorted, gesticulating at the strange corkscrew. "What in hell . . . !''

"Good God, let me see that,'' Hortense insisted, grabbing the instrument. "It looks like something from Star Wars. Don't tell me Basil gave you that?'' she sighed affectedly. "I think it's hydraulic and in any event needs more parts to make it operable, and Lord only knows where the parts are. Second drawer left of the fridge you'll find a sensible corkscrew.''

Much relieved, Ceese went to fetch it.

"And there's another box of funny-looking crackers on the counter, please.''

Sara managed to clear a space to sit down, and Hortense did likewise. She picked up an ancient-looking volume, checked its title, and sighed.

"Basil, you've still got Holinshed. You told Cyril you'd return it by the end of the week. It's going to get lost here among all these even sillier chronicles."

"Ah, glad you found it." Basil happily took possession. "Holinshed remains the single best collection of grizzly regicides and devious plots England has," he informed Ceese. "Of course, he's a capital plagiarist, but then who wasn't in those days?"

Ceese looked puzzled at this man of evident probity casually dismissing crime.

"Come now, my man. All this litigious folderol with copyright is the result of post-Renaissance individualism gone amuck. And too many lawyers." Basil waved his arm and pondered whether to lead on with a history of the copyright laws, the proliferation of attorneys compared internationally, or the original topic.

"Shakespeare himself, you must know, hadn't an original plot to his name. His lifted most from here," Basil announced, handing over the volume.

Ceese opened Holinshed's *Chronicles* with care and his eyes happened upon a particular horrific account of some quasi-historical event, but before he could grasp the whole scene, Hortense raised her wineglass on high.

"Here, here. I propose a toast!"

"You can take it with you," Basil urged Ceese, "just remind me to tell Dr. Prout. Some of it will make your hair stand on end."

"To the swift nabbing of the murderer!"

"Or murderers," Sara added.

"And book swipers," Ceese tossed in.

"And Tottel adders," Hortense caroled, heady from suspicious possibilities. "I'm willing to open the bidding on the identity of the murderer—one, for starters." She sat upright, ready to receive names.

"A moment, dear. May we establish a few rules? I particularly want us to rule out the psychopathic killer and either Mr. Boehm's or Mr. Moraise's death being a crime of passion."

"Agreed." Hortense felt she spoke for them all, having quickly surveyed Sara's ludicrous double take.

"Further, I suggest we exonerate those present of both murders—or shall we tick ourselves off one by one?"

"I'm the only one here who knew Leon, however remotely," Sara volunteered, "and you'll have to take my word for the time being. I'm sure I've got an alibi somewhere..."

"Given," Basil nodded generously. "But as for Mr. Moraise—we all knew him, at least by sight."

"That's not quite grounds for murder," Sara remarked, "and let's face it: of everybody here, I'm first in line for Giles as well. And I can't deny the thought often crossed my mind."

"What of that dour Ms. Gluck?" Basil speculated, grabbing up a cheese-slathered cracker.

"Ah, good. Now we're thinking creatively," Hortense cheered.

The timer on the microwave buzzed, aborting other incriminations. Basil rose to save the potatoes from disintegrating and Hortense suggested they repair to the dining room. As she distributed plates and cutlery at regular intervals, she speculated about the contemporary rage for serial murders.

"They evidence a paltry lack of imagination, if you ask me," she announced to Ceese as she handed him utensils.

At Basil's urging Ceese helped himself to a large portion of stew and was heavy into mastication as the others finished passing around the condiments. The pepper mill went untouched for lack of instructions as to its use.

"You know, I wouldn't be surprised if the book boggle has something to do with the murders. Now take that sixteen o eight third quarto Shakespeare published in sixteen nineteen but really after eighteen eighty. Let's not think for a minute that we stumbled on a singular case there," Hortense challenged the group, emphatically stabbing at something vivid on her plate. Basil halted with a forkful of mutton.

"Indeed. We've quite neglected that angle. I wonder if Cyril's aware—"

"Since he hasn't made it to the Renaissance, he pretends little knowledge and less responsibility. And when I told Giles," Sara said with some annoyance, "he was singularly disinterested. His nonchalance was nothing short of feckless."

"Certainly he couldn't have bashed himself on the head to cover up shady dealings?" Hortense imagined aloud.

"My dear, you may have landed on something. We know that Mr. Moraise was selling off items—the ones we purchased—and jacking up the prices to increase his purse for the Americana. Now it is evident that any extension of such practice begs for discovery. Whatever else he may have been, he could not have been stupid. To cover his tracks, he needed to replace at least some of the stolen volumes with—"

"Not Tottels, dear," his enthusiastic wife bellowed. "Why, we've no idea that Mr. Moraise has any clue about the Tottel additions. Ah, wait, we did mention them at that fellow Boehm's dreadful funeral."

"No, no, of course not the silly Tottels. But why not copies, or even cheap editions?" Basil's pale eyes squinted with devious possibilities.

Sara and Ceese's eyebrows raised in unison. Hortense was humming favorably.

"You know," she said slowly, "suppose he bought cheap copies. He could then sell off the genuine—oh, oh—better still," she spoke with mushrooming enthusiasm, "suppose he had copies custom-made and—well, distributed some as replacements, and perhaps tried to sell others to the unwary?"

"Dear, the messieurs at Sotheby's and their ilk are not unwary and certainly not likely to be fooled by forgeries. There *are* ways of knowing." Basil's authoritarianism was not fully settled in his gut. He wiped his mouth with his napkin and rose from his seat. He marched into the living room and returned with an old book in his hands.

"Thanks to Ceese's generosity, we've got the Higden back. See here, genuine G. van Os initials and all." Basil pushed aside his plate, dusted the crumbs from his place, and lovingly beheld the old edition.

Ceese was beaming and serving as attentive audience for any erudition that might fall his way. As neither Sara nor Hortense had pressing interest in the Higden, they began to clear the table.

"Ah, see here, Ceese, the Gothic influence yielding to...hmm. I hadn't noticed that before—these brown stains."

"Looks like them tea stains in that there other book—the old Shakespeare that turned out not to be so old."

"No, no. See here, well...wait a minute." Basil's gooseberry eyes popped as he bobbed his head to and from the volume. "Nooooo," he wailed at the ceiling.

A clatter of dishes in the kitchen followed Basil's pained outcry. Ready to grab Basil's gut for the Heimlich maneuver, Hortense came rushing in with Sara at her heels. They froze, waiting for a sign. Basil looked at them blankly. Hortense bent over to check for dilated pupils. Seeing the open Higden, she reassessed the situation. "Dear, isn't G. van Os all that he's cracked up to be?"

Basil remained blank, slowly casting his eyes down to the open page. He could say nothing.

"Oh, the famous musical notations," Hortense ran on, glancing at the page and hoping to spur a reaction in her husband. "The first in print, you know," she said pointedly to Ceese, "in England—or was it in the world, dear?"

"It's a forgery," Basil moaned under his breath.

Gasps were emitted from each of the onlookers.

"Are you certain? Look, those are G. van Os and there's the—"

"A forgery. A fake." Basil was recovering himself and removed his glasses so as not to be forced to see

the phony edition with any degree of clarity. He
rubbed the bridge of his nose with thumb and index
finger, sighed deeply, and sat back.

"Oh, it's a good one, I'll admit. A cursory glance
might even—did—fool the experts, but then again,
Higden isn't among the world's priceless treasures.
Sotheby's probably didn't bother with chemical tests
or ultraviolet light. In any event, this is not the Higden I examined at the Smedley a couple of months
back."

"Ya mean we got ourselves a fake?" Ceese asked,
just waking to the facts.

"I'm afraid so," Basil spoke, comforting himself
with recognition of Ceese's disappointment. "The
dead giveaway is here in the musical notations."

The three in the dark gave another look; two registered blanks; while the third, Hortense, whose musical abilities extended to construction and mastery of
a seventeenth-century model harpsichord, began
humming oddly.

"Hum, hom, hummm...oh, that's ghastly—not to
say unorchestrable for any instrument."

"Then you see my point. The Higden I examined at
the Smedley—the *real* Higden—drew upon Machaut's
motets. Rather pleasing selections, actually." Basil
drifted off into wistful reverie.

"Well, it doesn't take a musical genius to see that
these wretched measures couldn't have been com-
posed by Machaut or anyone with an ounce of musical sense."

"Quite so, my dear, quite so."

"Why do you suppose a forger would go to such
lengths to produce such good copy and then chuck the

whole effort with an absurd joke?'' Sara asked, unwilling to let go of a genuine work so easily.

"That may be it, Sara. A joke. A signature, a way of thumbing one's nose at the bibliographic world.''

"Well, all is not lost,'' Hortense insisted in an effort of revival. She was distributing spoons and cups of pulpy fruit. "The New York Public collects forgeries. They've a superb selection from the eighteenth century. Odd that the Enlightenment took to forgery with such abandon: Macpherson, Chatterton, Ireland—why, their immortality lies in their deceptions.''

"Ah, but, dear, they were creative forgeries,'' Basil awakened, "ones being passed off as new discoveries and really something of original works in their own right. Except perhaps Ireland's additions to the Shakespeare canon. Pure melodramatic bilge.''

"That's not entirely the case. There are some classic forgeries of first editions, though heaven knows with the careless practices of early printers and the Stationers' Register people—''

"I don't think we're making much progress into the murders,'' Sara said, distantly recalling the intended line of inquiry.

"Indeed. Check forgery. Other devious—hmm. Say, is it a genuine Aubusson?'' Hortense asked an indeterminate audience.

"Oh bisson what?'' Ceese asked, halting his spoon midair and staring at the purple puree.

"The carpet. The one Giles Moraise was lying on,'' Sara filled in, wondering why they were into carpets. "It's real, all right. Signed, dated, and numbered.'' Hoping to close off the topic, she added, "It cost a small fortune, but Giles insisted on it; he said the director of the Smedley had to have appropriate office furnishings—'furnishings commensurate with the position' were his words, as I recall.''

The general preference seemed to favor a new round of passing foodstuffs as opposed to pursuing Hortense's connection between carpets and means of demise. She, however, was not ready to drop what was a rich possibility.

"It does rule out suicide. Anyone who can appreciate a genuine Aubusson would not spill blood on it, especially his own.'' She was now satisfied.

"... AMONG WHOM WE HAVE the reference librarian, Ms.—''

"Sisson, *Miss*,'' the thin Winifred squeaked into the reporter's microphone.

"Oh, my God,'' Sara moaned as she, Cecil Blinn, and the Killingsleys stared at the TV screen. "I should have hung around to prevent this from happening.''

"And can you tell us, Miss Sisson, what happened—or why?''

Miss Sisson looked about ready to cry. "No,'' she snuffled.

The reporter was not pleased with the way the interview was going. "Anything strange at all at the Smedley?'' he pressed.

Apparently the word "strange'' triggered the terrified librarian's brain.

"Oh...oh, just about everything's strange. Books are getting stolen and others are being shelved that have no right—''

Sara was holding her mouth wishing it were Winifred's.

Fortunately the reporter wasn't interested in what he took to be normal library irregularities and tried to steer his interviewee toward murder. Miss Sisson, however, would have nothing to do with grisly death and merely shook and stuttered at its mention. The interview was mercifully brief.

"Well," Hortense sniffed and widened her eyes, pleased to have her suspicious proclivities popularized. Before she could say more, the reporter was back on the screen, this time with Ms. Gluck, who was forthcoming with Smedley strangeness.

"I tell you," she went on without prompting, "it's a wonder we're not all murdered at our stations. Though I'm with circulation and quite public, I have dreadful fears for the staff in remoter regions. You won't get me to linger in the stacks until these murders and thefts have been cleared up. Just the other day," Edwina was taking to her public informant role, "a couple of weird professors claimed to have discovered the theft of a rare book, Ranulf Higden's *Polychronicon*, you know?" Evidently the reporter did not know, did not care, and cut short this interview as well.

Basil and Hortense, however, not only cared, but were indignant at Ms. Gluck's pejorative characterization.

"To say nothing of her factual inaccuracy," Hortense added. "After all, I did not make then, nor do I now, any claims in the Higden affair. That was entirely Basil's doing, and while I shall not pretend indifference, my concern remains strictly marital. Especially as it is a forgery.''

Her antecedent, as her umbrage, was left to drift about the cluttered room.

TEN

THE PEOPLE AT SOTHEBY'S expressed clear and specifically directed umbrage when the Smedley contingent—Cyril Prout, Basil Killingsley, and Cecil Blinn—marched in on Friday morning with what was at best a bastardized copy of Higden's *Polychronicon*.

Mr. Curdleston, representing the bibliographic staff at Sotheby's, was well tutored in politic politeness. On the one hand, as he had explained on the telephone, the general rule of *caveat emptor* stood firm; on the other, no institution, however august, could long afford to have its service questioned, to have rumors bandied about as to its trafficking in shoddy merchandise.

"We do examine, you must be aware, all items in our purview and attempt to verify their authenticity as to whatever they purport to be. I say that because we have been known, quite legitimately, you understand, to act as agents for copies—occasionally famous forgeries." Mr. Curdleston raised his eyebrows and nodded to confirm the incredible. "Yes, indeed, there's a growing number of collectors of—well, shall we say, authentic copies of items? Furniture, jewels, and, yes, books. To be sure, the difference lies with intention: copy as flattery or felony, as we say." He folded his hands over his groin and rocked back on his heels.

"Yes, we understand, Mr. Curdleston, but all the same I am certain about this Higden. It's a fake, a felonious copy, if you will." Basil smiled politely.

"And we've proof," Cyril Prout inserted, ready to add starch to Basil's position. "Yes. A few days ago when Professor Killingsley told me his suspicions, I thought it worth checking with other libraries known to have the Higden edition. This morning I received photostats of the pages of musical notation in question from the British Museum."

Cyril reached into his leather portfolio and withdrew the papers. Basil opened the Higden to the corresponding page and lined up the texts. Ceese bent over to be the first to glean the truth.

"Don't look no different to me," he declared, ready to throw in the argumentative towel. "Just a bunch o' little dots running over the lines."

"Yes, but at different intervals, Ceese," Basil pointed out patiently. "The photostat's little dots translate as music—here, a couple of measures from a Machaut motet. My wife could tell you which one."

Mr. Curdleston looked impressed in an effort to gain time.

"However," Basil cleared his throat and pushed up his reading glasses, "that is beside the point. Dr. Prout admits ignorance in medieval music, but even he— even *he*—" Basil insisted to counter Ceese's naïveté in the matter, "acknowledges a variation in the placement of the little dots, as we are calling them. A variation, I need not add, of enormous consequence."

Mr. Curdleston examined the sets of musical bars and agreed that there was a discrepancy, though to what sonorous degree he was not prepared to say. Basil hummed each in turn, indicating with his pinky the precise note he was entuning.

Mr. Curdleston was not convinced so much by the quality of Basil's performance as he was by its earnestness.

"Hmm. We shall, of course, need to examine this under the lights. As you say, it's unlikely that this edition was simply off center at press. The notes are not congruent in any direction."

Basil looked pleased that his viewpoint was adopted. Cyril Prout did not look pleased. Ceese looked at the dots and silently hummed weird noises.

"You are aware, are you not," Mr. Curdleston continued in a businesslike manner, "that this volume is not the first, um, well, 'copy' that has reached us from the Smedley?"

The sinister implications of Mr. Curdleston's rhetorical question were not lost on the group.

"I haven't the foggiest notion what you mean," Cyril replied defensively.

"Well, sir, what I mean is that your director, Mr. Moraise, recently brought us a copy of—of—ah, yes, a Tyrwhitt Chaucer—"

Ceese blurted, "Ain't that Chaucer fella worth a million?"

Mr. Curdleston smiled. "I'm afraid not nearly that much. Upward of a few thousand, to be sure, in superb condition. In any event, though the bookplate authenticated the date, chemical examination of the glue revealed it to be Elmer's."

Cyril darted Basil a look of innocent horror.

"I informed Mr. Moraise of the situation and he, too, was quite taken aback. Several days later he re-

turned with another Tyrwhitt Chaucer." Mr. Curdleston folded his arms and removed a fleck of lint from
his navy blue sleeve. "Naturally, I thought it was curious that the Smedley would have two Tyrwhitts, of
whatever authenticity. I was under the impression that
the Smedley's is a small, but well-distributed collection, and thus I was suspicious of the duplication.
Rightfully so, I might add, for it, too, turned out to
be, shall we say, a lesser copy, one similar to but not
identical with the first? Equally worthless, however."

Cyril's jaw dropped lower and his forehead crinkled frantically. "But, but," he spluttered, "we do—
did—have a genuine Tyrwhitt Chaucer. I examined it
myself not two weeks ago. It was genuine. I assure
you."

"And so your Mr. Moraise thought. He was extremely disturbed—and rightfully so, I'd say, under
the circumstances..." Mr. Curdleston's voice trailed
off, and a not too veiled glance at his watch indicated
that his time was short. "We shall, of course, make
full restitution on this volume, as there is no question
of the Smedley's good faith in its purchase. We most
sincerely regret our part in the affair, though here, too,
we had no idea of the, well, soggy terrain on which we
were treading. The reimbursement will be forwarded
in due course."

None of the Smedley contingent found this to be
totally satisfying. Cyril was trying bravely to digest
another loss from his diminished empire; Basil's brain
was being tickled by unspecified resonance; and Ceese
was occupied with wondering who had dibs on the
Higden copy.

As the Higden loss and Tyrwhitt problem were being absorbed by the three men, the various women in and about the Smedley conducted themselves as they saw fit with regard to other bibliographic irregularities. Edwina Gluck at circulation was on a campaign to advertise the precarious nature of law and order at the library. She was convinced that only by openly disclosing every unfortunate instance could they hope to get back on the professional track.

"Excuse me, Dr. Tewksbury. I recognize how busy you are with the rampant murders and thefts around here, but I have no choice in calling your attention to another problem facing the Smedley."

Sara had not been pleased with Ms. Gluck's television debut, and now her effort to cry scandal on any pretext was becoming exasperating. She folded her arms over her chest and slumped, ready for Ms. Gluck's vitriol.

"One simply cannot ignore the findings of that Ms. Letty."

"Mrs. Leddy," Sara corrected.

"Mmm. In any event, she refuses to give over the specific information she says she has amassed about odd editions and *add*itions to the shelves. Ordinarily I'd dismiss her as a typical nuisance, one of the many we at general circulation must cope with, except for the fact that I have come across several strange volumes myself. I recall retrieving one such for that weird professor, the one with the buxom wife?" Edwina objectively evaluated her fingertips.

"You mean the Drs. Killingsley," Sara added to remind Ms. Gluck of proper address of patrons. "Yes,

I recall Professor Killingsley mentioning his surprise receipt of a Tottel's *Miscellany*, I believe?"

"That is correct. And I've seen several more of the same: legitimate call numbers, titles, and placement, but then that Tottel business inside. It is exceedingly disturbing." Ms. Gluck continued to scrutinize her outstretched fingers.

"Yes, Ms. Gluck, you were saying about Mrs. Leddy...?"

"Oh, her. I've tried to persuade her that *you* have better things to do than track down erroneous volumes—"

"How kind of you, Ms. Gluck, but as this Tottel business is getting out of hand and may be connected to other unorthodox happenings—"

"Murders and thievery, you mean."

"Possibly." Sara shifted her weight to one hip, deliberately toyed with her Indian totem necklace, and gave Ms. Gluck a look that suggested she cool it. "In any event, should you see Mrs. Leddy, you may tell her that I would be most pleased to speak with her."

Ms. Gluck raised her eyebrows, and recognizing the force of authority, however temporary and wayward it might be, gave a brief nod of assent and marched back to her station. On the way she maliciously tore off a leaf from Goodyear, the lobby's flourishing rubber plant.

"Did you see what that woman did?" Hortense Killingsley exclaimed as she approached Sara in the lobby. "It's been my theory that those who are short with people tend to expend their affections on the lower rungs of life's hierarchy. Evidently that woman has precious little concern for any living specimen."

Both women were rooted in Ms. Gluck's direction
with their hands planted in indignation on their re-
spective hips. Hortense's left hip was bulging under
her garden-green wraparound skirt. Tearing her gaze
from the incomprehensible Ms. Gluck, she twisted and
managed to extricate a small volume from her skirt
pocket.

"Oh, no, not you!" Sara drew back in mock horror. "Pocketing books from our dwindling collection!"

"However I may seem to be disgracefully engaged
in pilfering, the facts of the matter are quite the reverse." Hortense waved a little paisley-covered book
under Sara's nose.

"This was given to me by our comrade Mrs. Leddy
and represents her efforts to track down Tottel in two
of the three reading rooms: reference and periodicals,
I believe." Hortense opened the volume and held it at
a distance to read. "Hmm. Yes, the Z's are here and,
yes, the various periodicals…the *Journal of Waste and
Sewage Disposal*? Well, why not?" She perused the
pages with interest and continued expansively. "The
poor woman was in a dither to rid herself of what she
imagines is incriminating evidence. She went on about
being unable to locate you and refusing to give it over
to 'that Ms. Gluck,' as she called her. And so I became trusted agent of the goods."

"I see. Now all we need do is have our ersatz auditor check these out."

"Thee, not we. I have not had the fortune of meeting your new man, and so can be of no further use.
My linguistic luggage begs unpacking."

Hortense strode off to resume her scholarly rummage in the stacks, while Sara struck out to check the drains and hover outside lavatories in order to nab the new man.

As she turned to leave the lobby, she flipped open the little paisley book, did a rapid eenie-meenie-myniemo, and strode toward reference, fabric flowing and bangles clanking.

Winifred Sisson leapt up nervously from her desk, wringing her hands. She closed her glassy eyes and took a deep breath, willing herself to be calm.

"Oh, Dr. Tewksbury," she squeaked. "Can I help?" She spoke evidently in need of help herself. She was biting her lip and nearly drawing blood.

Sara noticed the frizzy pate of Basil Killingsley hunched over the serial catalogs and attributed Winifred's panic to his presence.

"Thank you, Miss Sisson, I suppose you may." Sara knew the distraction of business to be the best remedy for Miss Sisson's frazzled nerves. She handed over the paisley notebook and asked her to check out the call numbers from reference to see if they were what they purported to be.

"But why wouldn't they be?" Winifred's alarm sounded again.

"Mrs. Leddy—you know the lady who lurks around . . . ?"

"Oh—her—yes. Oh. The Tottels, you mean?" Winifred's eyes looked panicky.

"So you know about them?"

"Oh, no, not really," she hastily disclaimed. "Mrs. Leddy—she said she'd take care of it—that I needn't worry. And—well—I thought that as long as she wasn't *taking* anything from the room, and, well, she seemed so—well—occupied . . ."

Sara nodded kindly. "By the way, Miss Sisson, you haven't seen Herman Lobel around, have you?"

Miss Sisson started. "Who?"

"Never mind."

ELEVEN

"AUTHENTIC COPIES?" hooted Hortense in the quiet of the rare books room when she heard Basil, Cyril, and Ceese describe their interview with Mr. Curdleston at Sotheby's. "How oxymoronic! It does attest to, well, a host of phenomena, chief among which must be boredom!"

"Dumb, if you ask me," Ceese added. "People copyin' books they can't hardly make head nor tail of!"

Cyril Prout, caught in professional ambivalence between the need for strict definitions of authenticity and recognition of the role and importance of copies, nodded at the one and then the other. "The issue is to maintain the distinction. There are, for instance, less than five hundred extant Kelmscott Chaucers—"

"Three hundred ninety," Basil quietly asserted.

"Um, yes. I believe you're right. In any event, it's clear that such a work of art deserves wide dissemination and copies of Morris's extraordinary work—"

"Who's this here Morris fella?" Ceese asked, seeing an inlet to bibliognosticism.

Basil happily supplied information on William Morris, the Kelmscott Press, the edition of Chaucer produced therefrom, and a good deal more to dazzle Cecil Blinn's wits. With the number of Chaucers in the world multiplying, Ceese wondered where the Tyrwhitt Chaucer fit in, real or fake, that the Sotheby agent had mentioned.

"Thomas Tyrwhitt, my good man," Hortense spoke, eager to take up the instruction, "is a name much revered in literary and linguistic circles. Not only do we thank him for his edition of Chaucer, which, I need hardly add, salvaged the Father of English Poetry from virtual oblivion, but whose lucid (for the time) explication of Middle English versification single-handedly raised the tenor of medieval linguistic studies from that of eccentric enterprise to a major cognitive science." She paused and stood ready to take on opposition. Satisfied that the men were following with some degree of attentiveness, she continued. "Furthermore, Tyrwhitt serves as a splendid response to that wretched eighteenth-century proclivity for literary forgery. It was he, you may recall, who exposed the Rowley poems as forgery—even did an edition and found them quite superior specimens. Too bad the real author, Thomas Chatterton, didn't own up. He committed suicide, you know, at the tender age of seventeen. Tyrwhitt, thank heavens, had no part in that. The exposure was not till years later."

Hortense looked around for signs of flagging interest. Reading none, she went on with her literary gossip. "The exposure resulted from his work on Chaucer. Rowley, you see—the invented poet—was supposed to be a medieval monk. Arsenic, I believe...Chatterton's suicide, that is. In any event, the New York Public's got a strong holding of Tyrwhitt *and* of Rowley, né Chatterton."

"Thank you, dear," Basil spoke to turn off his burbling wife. "I believe we have the goods on Tyrwhitt."

"Ah, the goods!" Sara Tewksbury called as she approached Cyril Prout's desk waving a thick volume. "Here is the man—or his work—or a copy—itself. We've got only one—I can't imagine where Giles got two, or however many he had stashed away."

Ceese waved "hi" and increased the girth of his smile. He made outrageous mimetic gestures inviting Sara to lunch. She checked her watch, nodded, and passed the questioned volume to Cyril.

"Hmm, yes, that's puzzling," he noted, taking the proffered book. "The issue now is whether *this* volume is authentic, and if not..."

The shelf card for the Tyrwhitt Chaucer revealed it to have been purchased from a dealer, Acme Brothers, in 1984 for four hundred dollars. As it was getting on to lunchtime, the Killingsleys offered to drive Cyril to the downtown establishment. Cyril readily accepted, more hungry to get to the bottom of his Tyrwhitt than to the bottom of his lunch bag. All the way over to Acme Brothers, he busied himself with reasons for what he hoped was a gross underestimation of the volume's worth.

"Perhaps it was sitting around too long and the dealer simply wished to dump a low interest item? Perhaps he needed quick cash...?"

"Perhaps he's of questionable ethics?" Hortense skeptically added as they pulled up to the curb and scanned the decrepit storefront beneath the ACME BROS. sign. "A fence?" she whispered warily with a quizzical rise of her brow.

"It does look a bit, well..." Cyril conceded unhappily.

"Shady, I'd say," Hortense filled in as she squinted into the filthy window.

"We mustn't judge a book by its cover," Basil stiffly joked.

"Ah, but as Dickens says, 'There are books of which the backs and covers are by far the best parts,'" Hortense lightly challenged, not realizing the stake in Cyril's spirits.

"And with rare books one must," he sighed dejectedly just as an Acme brother opened the well-worn door.

"What can I do for you? Honest Abe Acme at your service." The potbellied figure bowed slightly. His ratty faded sport shirt was coming out of his pants as if the chance customer had rushed him from the facility.

Cyril Prout, seeing no need for elaborate social amenities, moved straight to the point as Honest Abe ushered them into the dusty store and feigned great interest in the Tyrwhitt tale. Inside, the tables and shelves were littered with piles of books haphazardly placed at all angles and directions.

"Ah, yes. We have lots of top-dollar volumes like the Tyrwhitt," Abe said, hiking up his pants.

"No doubt, but our interest is exclusively with this edition," Cyril spoke crisply holding out the book for inspection, "and with its previous owner."

Honest Abe's enthusiasm faded as he checked the title page. He picked up a cold cigar butt from a table's edge and stuffed it into his mouth muttering about his time being money. He looked around vaguely in a halfhearted attempt to locate the records, and shuffled off to a back room.

Cyril stood firm, trying not to touch the worthless junk that constituted Abe's visible inventory. Basil was craning his neck, looking up and around at the dirty shelves stuffed with books facing every which way. Hortense was nosing into the farther corners, lifting volumes here and there and stirring up little clouds of dust.

Honest Abe shuffled in from the dingy recesses with a grimy ledger open in his arms. He ran a cracked finger down the columns.

"Hmm. Oh here: Works of Chaucer edited by T. Tyrwhitt 1775–1778. That's a first edition," he snorted through his cigar, and looked down when the reassembled group was not duly impressed. "That asshole!" he snarled. "This guy here who sold me the book—if I ever get my mitts on him..." He turned the ledger around so Cyril could read the heinous name for himself.

"'Sebastian Crothers, ninety-two Ewell Street.' I'm afraid I don't know the fellow. Are you certain of his identity?"

"Look, I ain't called Honest Abe for nothing. I always get positive identification on the big stuff. But this asshole ain't living there anymore. If you find him, just let him know I'm looking for him."

"My, whatever did he do to so incur your wrath?" Hortense asked as if she were in league with the offensive party.

"The guy's into direct dealing—trying to cut honest guys like me out of making an honest living. And some of his stuff ain't on the up-and-up. I ain't gonna

be used as a fence," he spoke, shaking his dirty finger
in Cyril's direction. "Not Honest Abe."

"Well, um, yes." Cyril went on copying. "Yes, this
is it: sold to G. Moraise, two hundred dollars, July
seventh, eighty-four."

"The shelf card said—" Hortense clamped shut her
mouth.

Basil again looked at his wife meaningfully and
hastened to capitalize on Abe's acerbity.

"Um. I gather, Mr. Acme, that you haven't seen
much of this Crothers fellow lately?"

Honest Abe screwed up his eyes so that his cigar
butt stuck straight out. "Like I says, I got my eye out
for him. He used to bring in a steady flow of quality
stuff—some of it real good and some of it good
enough to pass—but I don't deal in shit," he added
hastily. "Naw, the guy tried to cross me once, but I let
him know I was on the up-and-up as I says."

"And have you had other dealings with this
G. Moraise?"

The down-and-out book dealer gave the matter
thought. "Can't say's I seen much of him neither since
about the time of that scum Crothers. And as I rec-
ollect, he used to come in fairly regular. I dunno, I'd
have to check the books." Abe Acme didn't appear
ready to spring into action unless compensated and/or
compelled by legal necessity.

When the group returned to the Smedley, the discrepancy between the shelf card purchase price and
Honest Abe Acme's ledger was another last straw for
Sara Tewksbury. Even the glow from her mint julep
lunch with Ceese could not muster civility to the dead.

"I was never a big fan of Giles's, but I never thought him that sleazy," she moaned, sweeping back her frazzled hair.

"Villainous!" Hortense assented solidly. "However, for all practical purposes he's dead and we might think about getting a line on this Sebastian Crothers fellow. He seems to be a crony in spirit and probably in fact."

"Which," Basil picked up the thread of his wife's argument, "may not necessarily help us with the problem raised by the gentleman at Sotheby's—that Mr. Moraise was, perhaps unwittingly, offering forged copies of Tyrwhitt as genuine first editions. Furthermore, this edition, Cyril here has assured us, is genuine."

"It is," Cyril insisted as if another treasure were going to be robbed from his collection. "Watermarks, ligatures, signatures—not a suspicious aspect to it. Its only flaw is this one large inkblot." He opened the volume for the group's inspection.

Basil studied the too regular reddish-black stain.

Hortense scanned the text above and below.

"Curious shape and placement. It looks like rich pickings for a Rorschach fan. Evidently it's been blotted and oh, of course! Basil, page a hundred and one!" She definitively announced the obvious fact to the larger audience. Ceese looked puzzled until Sara filled him in on the more or less universal practice of placing library imprints on the hundred and first page.

"You mean the book's been filched?"

As no one seemed inclined to contradict the logical leap, Ceese continued to plow down this felonious path. "But suppose a liberry wanted to sell a book that had its stamp already?"

Again Sara furnished the information, explaining the several legitimate ways of transferring ownership, inkblotting not being among them. "The point is, whoever blotted this page either isn't too bright or else felt that the purchaser wouldn't be. Ordinary ultraviolet light can read through ink."

"I'd say both." Hortense huffily responded to the previous point but one. "That Crothers fellow—and your late director as well—seems to have had more self-interest than professional integrity."

Cyril Prout, reminded that another treasure might be snatched from his grasp, sighed heavily. Feeling duty-bound to uncover the Tyrwhitt's legal ownership, he slumped off in Hardyesque gloom with the volume cradled in his arms.

Sara summoned her administrative will to carry on affairs in the shrinking library, and Hortense, too, marshaled her wits for the task of following through on what was becoming a nearly certain drift of T's to D's in the fifteenth-century northwest Midlands, and, if she kept on target, might well prove to have roots in specific continental labial developments of preconquest days. The merest hint of William the Conqueror's (on the whole overrated) effects on medieval England spurred Basil back to the stacks to pursue his feudal economic concerns and their imperialistic offshoots. Ceese, without professional purpose, reckoned he'd follow and learn more about liberry operations.

Ceese trailed Basil up to the sixth-level stack where the B 200s of philosophy were shelved. Most of these were large compendia of works: *The History of Philosophy* in twenty volumes, or *Western Thought from Plato to the Present* in equally formidable bulk. Ceese moved to the next archive where individual volumes were housed, and while Basil hunted down the Thomistic view of the feudal world, Ceese's roving eye caught a bright red text, which he pulled from the shelf. He flipped it open and read: "The question is raised in the subjective development of subjectivity to which negative employment of the extenuated dialectic possesses the remarkable trait that systematically cannot be maintained."

Ceese screwed up his eyes, reread the passage, and repeated a few of the thorny phrases. He couldn't imagine a situation in which this nonsense would be applicable. This was certainly not a Tottel poem. He smirked at his own humor. He spoke aloud, "subjective development of subjectivity..." shutting his eyes as if his ear alone might penetrate the sense his eye had not. When Ceese came to his commonsensical self, a tall, lanky fellow with a hook nose was standing in front of him. He had on baggy trousers.

"Ah! A man after my own heart, soaking up a bit of midafternoon Kierkegaard. One of my favorite savants. Barely makes a stitch of sense and uses so much yarn. That, my good sir, is genius."

Basil looked up from Volume 12 of the *Summa Theologica* (specifically Question 26 on The Order of Charity wherein he hoped to find some rung relegated to the lord-vassal relationship), and looked through the bookshelves, the space giving partial visibility of the party addressing Ceese.

The party stood tall, beaming into space, while Ceese peered at the curiosity, unsure if a response was called for, and less sure of what an appropriate one might be.

"Actually," the lanky fellow went on, "it doesn't matter—Kierkegaard, Erigena, Ockham, Plato, Locke, Wittgenstein, you name it—" Ceese was glad he didn't have to "—they all expound beyond solid context."

Before Ceese could decide whether to agree or just maintain a heavy, thoughtful look, the loquacious fellow went on. "I mean, the sense of perception of ideas—for us, you and I, through the printed page, the text in its wholeness, its entirety, its integrity." He gazed off beyond solid context.

Was this philosophy or lunacy?

Even Basil Killingsley who had more than his share of philosophy, and lunacy, in his background, came up short. He gave the cloudy matter some thought and was about to toss in the Thomistic perspective to clarify the fact that nothing new has happened since 1500, when the somewhat theatrically pitched voice introduced itself to Ceese. "Name's Crothers. Sebastian Crothers."

Ceese heard distant resonance in the name, but Sebastian, having conceded a moment to solid context, raced back to the metaphysical or wherever he was heading.

"Editions: fascinating histories, worlds unto themselves," he went on, conscious that his captive audience judged him lunatic. A secondary thought crossed his mind that, given the hefty build of the fellow, he was better off being labeled lunatic than gay.

Basil, inured to sophomoric gibberish, was, however, annoyed by the persistence of this fellow's tone. Of course he was addressing Ceese, whose intellectual intimidation level was low. Perhaps he ought to step in and rescue the good-natured Smedley benefactor?

The lanky ersatz philosopher continued his act. "Yes, *objets d'art*, bearing their own as well as Man's immortality and Man, the supreme and ephemeral egotist, values them as if scarcity constituted worth!"

"Cecil Blinn here. Ceese to my friends," Ceese insisted, as if this bit of civility might calm the excited fellow.

"Ah, Texan? I wouldn't think philosophy and oil mixed. But then, philosophy doesn't mix with much of solid context, as I said. That's what made me move to the *study*, *acquisition*, *duplication*, and *creation* of text." He thumped his index finger in the direction of Ceese's nose. *"Context,"* he repeated with an oversized grin revealing small, straight teeth.

"You don't say?" Ceese noticed the fellow's large trouser pockets. They seemed to be stuffed with books.

"Hmm. What astounds me—what truly amazes and astounds—is the subjective value placed on text—*not*, I must stress, based on intrinsic intellectual content that could be had identically in a two-ninety-five paperback—not that many philosophers are worth that," Sebastian chuckled and winked at his compulsory confidant.

Again Basil looked up from his text. Although the oddball lecturing Ceese was, well, vigorous in his verbiage, there was something of a viewpoint emerging from his cluttered speech. Was not his point in the vicinity of Basil's own view on rare books?

Ceese leaned against the shelves with putative interest as if a kernel might be gleaned in the nut.

"No, worth lies in such artificial and ultimately meaningless factors as age and scarcity. The same text—well," Sebastian reached over and plucked out a Boethius from the shelf opposite, "*this* in an early Renaissance edition would—"

"Like an incunabulum?" Ceese proudly tossed out.

Basil smiled and nodded into the *Summa*. Ceese was catching on. He was doing just fine on his own handling the loquacious fellow. The professor picked up the thread of Thomas's argument and quietly carried it to a carrel.

"That's it, old chum, yes, an incunabulum of Boethius—virtually unreadable, I need hardly add—is bought and sold for thousands, whereas a perfectly readable paperback—well, you see my point?"

Ceese nodded in some sympathy.

"I'll tell you—there's something bizarre in such a value system. Especially when a good deal of the time the experts can't distinguish between a real first edition, and a, well, um, *doctored* one."

For a split second Ceese stopped nodding and smiling. Sebastian, however, was so taken with his own argument that he didn't notice.

"And yet," he again extended his pointer finger, "collectors, dealers, and even library directors will pay through the teeth for scarcity. It's not art; it's not content; it's not utility. You know what it is?" Sebastian's finger was close to poking Ceese's broad chest. "It's vexatious superbity—greed calling itself economics—atrocious, vulgar values!'' He had reached his crescendo of ventilation, which apparently served to satisfy him.

Ceese tried to look thoughtful at the onslaught of wisdom hurled in his direction.

"You think about it," Sebastian concluded as his eye caught a volume just to the left of Ceese's head. He reached over and pulled it off the shelf. Waving goodbye to the stranger, he turned and flipped open the book. He grinned broadly.

Ceese could have sworn that the bold-lettered title page had on it the name of Tottel.

TWELVE

WHILE BASIL WAS ENGAGED in the Thomistic tapestry of arguments, articles, and questions, and Ceese was engaged in the context of Sebastian Crothers's idiocy, Sara Tewksbury ran into a lesser variety of existential bewilderment in the persons of Edna Leddy and Hortense Killingsley.

"P'sst, Dr. Tewksbury, I'm glad I caught you!"

"Hello, Mrs. Leddy. How's the hunt going? And Professor Killingsley?"

"You'll never guess!" Hortense burst forth. "Mrs. Leddy is a virtual magnet for Tottels. Just look at the pages of call numbers she's amassed. Why, I'd hire her instead of that Lobel fellow no one seems to be able to find!"

Edna pursed her lips and looked down shyly. "I didn't want to bother *you* and so I was just telling Professor Killingsley..."

Hortense's chesty pride in a co-conspirator's scrupulosity was checked by dudgeon—dudgeon at the woman's assessment of whose time is worth what—but Edna was oblivious. She glanced over her shoulder for spies and went on. "Today we—M. Farb and I—we spent several hours in the stacks and things aren't so bad there," she confided, leaning sideways to Sara's torso and half concealing her mouth. "Three in about—um," Edna opened her new notebook and counted down a page, "seven aisles, both sides. And one wasn't a Tottel; it was an edition of—mm, let me see—oh, here: Francis Meres's *Palladis Tamia*. The text looked just like Tottel's with all those little poems in old English. But it wasn't,'' she concluded emphatically, snapping shut the notebook.

"Ah, a *Palladis Tamia*!" Hortense sang, dropping her dudgeon and vitiating Edna's attempts at secrecy. "How novel! I am glad to hear the fellow has expanded his horizons. Tottel does wear on one."

Sara smirked and nodded encouragingly to Edna. As she was about to express yet again her appreciation for Mrs. Leddy's help, out of the corner of her eye she spotted movement faintly issuing Herman Lobel vibes. She touched Edna Leddy's shoulder for pause, and discreetly called out the infamous name. The khaki legs of the body loosely associated with the name Herman Lobel came to a halt just around the corridor's corner. There was a moment of silence, and a sneaker-shod fellow bent around the wall's edge.

"Who me?"

"*You,* Herman Lobel."

No sooner had he come full forward than Edna Leddy let out a timid gasp and grasped Sara's arm for stability.

"*That* is Herman Lobel?" she whispered incredulously.

"God, I hope so," Sara sighed.

"But, Dr. Tewksbury—"

"Well, Herman," Sara broke in to greet the long-lost auditor.

"Hi." Herman waved foolishly to Sara and nodded to the other two women as if they were long-standing neighbors.

Edna's mouth was agape in modified horror, while Hortense was screening the lumpy fellow with scholarly curiosity. So, here was the new chief auditor. She recalled that as Leon Boehm hadn't been *au courant* in his methods, one could scarcely expect much from this fellow, his inauspicious appearance notwithstanding.

Sara continued, keeping fairness in mind. "Herman, I know the auditor's job was, well, thrust on you with little warning," Herman nodded appreciatively, "and you may not know all the ropes" (Herman smiled at the sympathetic understatement), "but even you must admit that the job won't get done—we're not mentioning quality—the job won't get done if you're never here."

Herman was trying to ascertain the degree, if any, of irony masked by his boss's surface patience and reasonableness. Edna was doing her best to be inconspicuous behind the assistant director's gauzy torso while scrutinizing the gelatinous features of Herman Lobel.

"I want you in my office, Herman," Sara checked her watch and frowned, "Monday, at nine A.M. Nine sharp." She swiftly turned 180 degrees so Edna's face was grazed by her braless breasts and ropes of beads and other neck hangings of dubious ornamental worth. Edna, however, was equally eager to escape the perplexed fellow and so did her own about-face to march off with her comrade. Hortense stood blinking in disbelief at the sample of youth represented by the fellow slumping off, hands in pockets.

While perplexity concerning the specifics of his carpet call were tumbling in Herman's untidy brain as he shuffled off to his newly refurbished apartment (not quite *Architectural Digest*, but the pieces from National Office Furniture Suppliers did have a certain cachet), a host of potential threats were gaining substance in the mouth of Edna Leddy as she attempted to keep pace with Sara Tewksbury.

"Dr. Tewksbury," she gasped as the Mutt and Jeff pair strode down the corridor, "why, you *know* who that man is?"

Sara looked strangely at Edna, chiefly because she found it odd hearing Herman Lobel referred to as a man.

Hortense remained rooted to the spot and shifted her mental gears. One gear turned to the time: it was nearly five and she ought to finish up Grimm's Law, at least as far as the fourteenth-century northwest Midlands were concerned; another greasier gear turned to Mrs. Leddy who, however feckless of a scholar's time she might be, did seem unduly agitated. Or was she duly? Hortense uprooted her espadrilles and followed the acting director and her accomplice.

She caught up as Edna burbled her revelation. "He's—he's—oh, my goodness," Edna clutched her bosom and immediately stiffened to summon her reserves, "why he's the very person who's been putting the Tottels on the shelves!" She heaved a sigh of relief, having successfully executed her difficult task.

Hortense nearly hooted at the manifold ironies the identification instantly revealed (at least to her way of thinking), whereas Sara merely voiced an appropriate "well, well, well." For her the chief irony was that

Herman's culpability only served to elevate him in her estimation.

Edna went on busily to describe the particulars of how and when she observed Herman going about his distributions. As she was finishing her precise account, they were joined by Monsieur Farb, who, though he could not confirm the identity of Herman Lobel in the latter's physical absence, nonetheless spoke eloquently on Madame Leddy's behalf.

"Mais oui," he went on in what Sara swore was a thicker French cadence than he had in Smedley board meetings, "Madame is *très formidable* at the task. And it is so dry in the stacks, *non*? Madame and I—we are going for something to refresh ourselves, to moisten the palate, *n'est-ce pas*? Perhaps, mesdames," he bowed slightly to Sara and then Hortense, "you would care to join us? You will be welcome."

"Sorry," Hortense declined, "but Grimm's calling. Fricatives and plosives and all that, you know."

"Thanks," Sara also nodded, "but I've got a million things to check on before packing it in. You two go on and enjoy yourselves. You've been doing yeomen's service around here."

As she turned back toward her office and Hortense headed for reference, Sara wondered what Monsieur Farb was going to report to the Smedley board about the Tottels *et alii*. He had always been so reserved at meetings, more of the quiet gentleman's club sort à la Maurice Chevalier, but who knew what lurked beneath a simple exterior? After all, look at pimply Herman Lobel. Well, she would have to do just that Monday morning and she might as well use the opportunity to discuss not only his laxity on the job, but also what could be viewed only as fiduciary sabotage: the addition of illegitimate material to the Smedley shelves. Which reminded her to see how Miss Sisson was getting on with Edna's listing of reference room Tottels.

Though it was a half hour after staff quitting time, Miss Sisson was still flapping around among the reference archives not quite alone (Hortense's implosions echoing from one aisle), but quite distraught. She was frenetically turning pages in the paisley notebook and making frantic stabs at the shelves. When Sara caught up with her, Winifred nearly leapt from her skin in surprise.

"Oh. Dr. Tewksbury, it's you."

"Yes, Miss Sisson. It is I. I see you've been checking out the call numbers Mrs. Leddy listed. How's it going?"

"Oh, terrible. There must be something wrong. I can't find several of these numbers—or else they're not what they're supposed to be. I'm being very careful—"

"I'm sure you are," Sara said to mollify the wrungout Winifred. "No one's blaming you. Besides, these books weren't supposed to be on the shelves in the first place." Sara took the notebook and saw that Winifred had industriously double-checked the list and a few items had two X marks next to them. Just to test out her own grasp of reality, Sara looked up a few nearby numbers.

Among the nearby numbers Hortense was forming fricatives left and right. She snapped shut the volume in her possession and grabbed another.

"Not a Tottel, is it?" Sara queried seriously.

"No," Hortense checked the spine, keeping her finger in place, "it's what it purports to be."

"That's odd," Sara remarked as she checked the volumes adjacent to the shelf space Hortense's selection had made. Hortense recognized Edna's paisley notebook in Sara's grasp.

"You mean things aren't as Mrs. Leddy indicates? Have you done her whole list?"

"Miss Sisson has. I was just double-checking to make sure everything that's listed is either there or not as she marked."

Standing in feverish anticipation in the free space of the reference room with nothing but worry to cling to, Miss Sisson heard Sara's confirmation of the new-found confusion.

"Oh, dear. Whatever can have happened, Dr. Tewksbury?"

Sara shrugged and was as calmly baffled as Winifred was panicky. With a few words of comfort and support, Sara urged Winifred to go home. Hortense checked her watch and figured to do the same.

"Indeed, my fourteenth-century fricatives will remain where they are, I hope. Right now I'd best locate Basil or we'll be missing more than unwanted Tottels. *Au revoir,* as we seem to be saying around here."

"I've had it," Sara wearily agreed. She just wanted to go home and forget about bodies, Tottels, numbers, and incompetence. Monday would be soon enough to deal, beginning at 9 A.M. with Herman Lobel. If he appeared.

Sara again headed in the direction of the office to drop off Edna Leddy's notebook. Was Mrs. Leddy a nut, too? How could there be such discrepancy between her listed numbers and what was on the shelves? How could she confront Herman Lobel with adding unauthorized material to the shelves when the material in question wasn't always there? Her thoughts were curtailed by familiar dulcet tones from down the hall.

"Ah, and here she is now," Hortense announced with all the flourish of a talk-show emcee. "I said you were still about. Basil's been boring poor Ceese through the floorboards with Holinshed's *Chronicles*."

"Dear, Ceese and I were having a perfectly scintillating conversation about some of the more florid episodes of English regal history."

"You know some of them stories are real grizzly?" Ceese said earnestly. "I been reading them and there's some that's enough to make your scalp crawl . . ."

"But as I was telling Ceese, we must consider Holinshed to be something of a hack, a stitcher of others' cloth. Most of his so-called chronicle comes from Hall's bombastic history, who, of course, lifted wholesale from Polydore Vergil's even more pompous Latin history of England."

"Dear, Sara is not—"

"This chronicle, you may be pleased to know, does not begin *ab ovo*, as do the medieval accounts, but *ab inundata*. There's something to be gleaned from that." Basil had tickled his professional fancy and was ruminating on scholarly possibilities.

"Yes, dear, perhaps you've a kernel to chew for long winter nights. Meanwhile, we are being rude to

Sara here, who's no doubt got quite enough conundra for her summer entertainment.''

Sara smiled in acknowledgment of the understatement. Nonetheless, she realized that civility demanded that the group be invited into her office.

''Grab a chair and fill me in on the latest mayhem.''

''We'll be just a moment,'' Basil murmured, deftly aware from Hortense's gestures that perhaps the both of them were intruding on the other couple's weekend. ''We—or rather *I* am here with information of genuine pertinence.''

With the sense that to the Killingsleys (either and both) everything had pertinence to something or other, Sara resigned herself to a circumlocutory half hour, after which, she could tell, Ceese would press her for dinner. Well, why not? She threw herself into Giles's rich leather swivel chair and leaned back luxuriously.

When the rest of them were tentatively stationed on the edge of seats, Basil continued in businesslike fashion. ''I have just left Cyril Prout and he reports that infrared light was indeed able to penetrate the inkblot on the Tyrwhitt Chaucer. This Tyrwhitt, it turns out, was owned by the New York Public, *but*,'' Basil dramatically emphasized, ''*they* claim that their three Tyrwhitt Chaucers are all accounted for and haven't left the confines of midtown Manhattan since the war. Cyril didn't ask which war, but as my wife is fond of saying, those of us of a certain generation know which war was The War.''

''Dear, you're dithering.''

Basil looked at his wife and recognized priggish satisfaction in noting her characteristic fault in others.

"Well, Cyril is understandably puzzled as to how the New York Public can account for its holdings when clearly one of them has been stolen and is here, on whatever pretext, in the Smedley."

"Perhaps it's something in the air that causes a rather amazing multiplication of texts? What with the Tottels proliferating like rabbits, and now—"

"The number of Tyrwhitts is not the issue. The New York Public's got its three and the Smedley has its one," Basil added with a hint of impatience.

"Don't forget that Giles offered two to Sotheby's—and both were later and lesser editions than ours," Sara clarified.

"Hmm," Basil responded, not happy to be stumped.

"There was this fella in the stacks," Ceese began, not fully appreciating the stump, having veered off at the mention of Tottel, "a sort of weirdo I met this afternoon and I think he was goin' off with one of them Tottels."

"Herman Lobel?" Sara asked with interest, not sure if Ceese could recognize the Smedley auditor.

"Nope. Fella by the name of..." Ceese crinkled his brow and rubbed his chin. "Darn. Professor, did ya catch his name?" Basil pondered, and nodded to the negative. "I remember he was goin' on about text and *con*text and editions and wavin' his arms a lot, and not makin' a whole lot of sense. He was a mite screwy, you know?" Basil nodded in the affirmative. "Also threw in somethin' about doctorin' books."

The condition of the fellow's nuts and bolts was not nearly as riveting as doctored books in the Smedley context. The three looked encouragingly at Ceese, urging him to recall further details.

"Lemme see. He said he was a philosopher and— oh—he said somethin' about incunabulum—that's right—and that nobody bein' able to tell a real one from a fake—'doctored,' he said."

Sara, Basil, and Hortense were upon Ceese trying to midwife his recollection of the fellow's name.

"A? B? C? D?" Hortense thrust the alphabet piecemeal at the pondering Texan.

"C...B..." Ceese mulled and suddenly brightened. "Sebastian Bothers."

Basil's frizzy brows jutted toward Ceese. "Bothers? Or was it Crothers?"

"Yahoo, that's it! Say, how did ya know?"

Hortense and Basil gaped at each other in wondrous recognition. Sara, like Ceese, had some vague resonance from the name, but couldn't place it.

"Ninety-two Ewell Street," Basil informed the two blank faces. "But he's moved." As the tidbit failed to stimulate the expected epiphany, Basil tossed out the whole kernel.

"He sold a Tyrwhitt Chaucer to Honest Abe Acme who, in turn, sold it to one Giles Moraise."

"Oh!" The blank faces lit up in unison.

The fitting together of these few facts only encouraged the three to several other varieties of mnemonic games.

"Sorry, folks, my brain's dried up. Maybe," Ceese smiled innocently at Sara, "a few mint juleps, a nice big dinner...?"

"Oh, thanks, Ceese, but Basil and I promised ourselves an evening of marathon VCR viewing. We're going to fast forward a half dozen documentaries—it cuts down to a thirty-four-minute hour! And the microwave will defrost stuffed jalapeño peppers—"

"Dear, neither Ceese nor Sara is interested in our dinner menu."

"Of *course*. How silly of me. Though they are red jalapeños from Texas."

"Come along, dear."

THIRTEEN

AT 9:20 MONDAY MORNING when Herman Lobel had still not shown up, Sara went out to the lobby with the vain hope that searching would have some effect on his appearance. Looking about in anticipation, she herself was spotted by the prim and efficient Edna Leddy. When Sara mentioned the discrepancy between Edna's recorded Tottel call numbers from reference and the fewer texts on the shelves, Edna was appalled, then baffled, then outraged. Suddenly she clapped her hand over her mouth and disappeared behind an adjacent pillar.

"It's him," she whispered, barely moving her thin lips.

Sara turned and saw Hortense Killingsley bobbing questions at Herman Lobel. He was moving sluggishly, trying to deflect the large woman's barrage.

"It's all right, Mrs. Leddy. Herman's harmless, and so is Professor Killingsley, I think."

Edna looked doubtful, but reluctantly emerged from her hideout.

"Halloo!" Hortense bellowed as if coming upon Dr. Livingstone in the jungle. "Look what I found! The new auditor! I was just filling him in on the deplorable swivel chair tallies—!"

Sara nodded.

"Mr. Lobel, over here. I'd like you to meet another very special Smedley patron, Mrs. Leddy."

"Hi. Yeah. I've seen you around."

Edna was surprised that her invisible cloak was nothing of the sort, especially to its chief target.

"Mrs. Leddy, you might be interested to know, has been a great follower of yours," Sara said, amusing only herself.

Herman scratched his cheek. "Huh?"

"Mrs. Leddy, Herman, has been tracking down your silly placements of Tottel's *Miscellany* and recording their random locations."

Herman smiled and then grinned. "No law against donating."

Hortense looked aghast. Today's youth were ever upping the ante of gall.

Sara, closer to the generation, knew the line had been planned.

"Herman, I don't really care why your generosity seeks such strange outlet. That it does, well, disrupt library cataloging and auditing is my concern—and should be yours. However," she spoke with casualness emulating boredom, "the problems your Tottels—"

"Not just Tottels, though mostly," Herman added for proper accreditation.

"Ah, yes," Hortense interrupted. "Francis Meres's *Palladis Tamia*, I believe, has made a modest showing?"

Herman smiled.

"Yes. We know." Sara acknowledged both ditty fans. "As I was saying, the problem seems to be clearing itself. I've just been telling Mrs. Leddy that from last check yesterday, many of your foolish additions have disappeared from the shelves."

Herman looked puzzled. His face clouded.

"That shit Sebastian," he muttered, loud enough for Mrs. Leddy to hear "shit," Sara, "Sebastian," and Hortense both "shit" and "Sebastian."

"Ah, Mr. Crothers," Hortense announced as if she were an intimate of his; after all, how many Sebastians could there be?

Herman was grinding his teeth and clenching his fists in a parody of pugilism.

"Herman, I suggest we take ourselves to—"

"Psst," Edna hissed, having restationed herself behind the pillar.

"Yes, Mrs. Leddy?"

Edna beckoned so that her secret would be revealed to none but the authorities. Sara rolled her eyes upward.

Hortense recognized Sara's reluctance to let Herman Lobel out of sight.

"Ah, Dr. Tewksbury, do let me. I believe I'm numbered among Mrs. Leddy's trusted cohorts."

"Thanks. Herman, we are going straight to my office."

Hortense slithered up to Edna, hoping to engage her conspiratorial proclivities.

"Aha! Another felon spotted, Mrs. Leddy?" she spoke through slit lips.

Edna looked at Hortense, again deciding the buxom professor would do in the pinch.

"That's him."

"Who?"

"Over there. The one with the baggy trousers."

"I see, but who is he?"

"I don't know, but—oh, we mustn't let him get away." Edna clutched Hortense's thick, moist arm.

"I agree. Quite suspicious, Mrs. Leddy, but let's keep calm. Who is he and why shouldn't we let him get away?"

Edna swallowed hard and collected herself.

"I don't know his name, but on several occasions—at least three or four times—I've seen him put books in his pockets. He was stealing!"

For a split second Hortense was as puzzled and shocked as Edna, but then quickly sorted out the various facts. One was that while Smedley security wasn't all that it should be, even with kindly old Cribbs at the main door, the amateur would be detected by the metal sensors bound in every volume. Unless, of course, the books didn't have the sensors because they were illegitimate placements, which meant that there was Herman Lobel's "shit Sebastian." It was worth a try.

Hortense indicated that Edna might keep guard at the pillar while she, the brawn of the team, pursued the baggy-trousered fellow. She carried her person swiftly across the lobby on rubber-soled espadrilles that squelched on the marble floors. Ms. Gluck's disapproving ear was activated. The frivolous squeaks constituted a serious violation of the spirit of library law; however, as she could not cite the letter against shoe squelches, she was left to raise her eyebrows and glare at the ill-shod offender.

"Excuse me, Mr. Crothers?" Hortense called.

Sebastian had just rounded the edge of the circulation desk and flashed his stack pass at Ms. Gluck. He hadn't heard his name, though Ms. Gluck certainly had.

"Excuse me, Mr. Crothers." Hortense spoke with certainty, this time halting Sebastian.

"Could I see you for a moment?"

"Me? By all means, take a good look. Have we a basis for acquaintance?"

Ms. Gluck edged over to within reach of the conversation and the silent alarm button. She gave a signal indicating her full cooperation should the fellow become violent. Hortense, however, read Edwina's pinched-faced contortions as characteristic disapproval and grimaced. Ms. Gluck shuddered and pulled her prune face in further.

"Mr. Crothers, we have not formally established a basis for acquaintance, but I should like to do so. If you don't mind, would you please follow me to the director's office? The lobby really isn't a good place to discuss private matters," she said, thereby informing Ms. Gluck of her exclusion.

"Oh? No acquaintanceship and yet we have private matters to discuss. How very odd."

Hortense's thirty-three years among occasional snotty youth had taught her a thing or two.

"If you'd rather not come along quietly, I can have the security officer help you." She indicated Cribbs at the entrance, hoping that Mr. Crothers was not on to his decorative status.

Ms. Gluck, still all ears, placed her finger on the underdesk alarm button in readiness. Regardless of the professor's rudeness, Edwina would do her duty.

"Oh. It's come to that," Sebastian said with huffy petulance.

"Not unless you choose." Hortense was quite up to her authoritative stature.

"Very well, but frankly I can't see what you want with me."

As the two passed by the pillar inadequately concealing Edna Leddy, Hortense slowed down and signaled that Edna should feel free to go about her business. After all, the confrontation of donor and thief seemed enough to keep the ball of confusion going.

By the time Hortense and Sebastian reached the office, not only did they find the surprised face of Herman Lobel, his pink, pockmarked countenance reflecting every vacillation in mood, but the numbers were swollen by Basil Killingsley, who was aggressively discussing some thorny point with Sergeant Kinney, who had his notepad flipped open, having yet again identified the frizzy-haired professor and yet again established his essential ignorance in matters of import to the police.

"Look who we have here!" Hortense bellowed after assessing the room's occupants. No one was sure to whom the "who we have here" referred, but she rushed on in her own train. "Sergeant Kinney, I believe. At last might we see something approaching an investigation? If I might be of service with a few obvious pointers?"

Without encouragement Hortense blathered on connecting the deaths of Leon Boehm and Giles Moraise with the unorthodox shifts in rare books. Though her explanations were having their persuasive effect on Basil, the sergeant didn't seem impressed or even interested. Herman's slack jaw was still ajar, while

Sebastian was appearing as if it were some huge joke that he of all people should be in this administrative office. Sergeant Kinney levered himself forward and back staring at the air above the Killingsleys' heads.

"Well" was the best Sara could come up with until the basic civilities sorted themselves out. What clicked into place was a sense that the group's sparks of confrontation might ignite into illuminating flames. Who knew where idle egotism or silly incomprehensibility might take them?

The nominal introductions established no common ground, though the Killingsleys were pleased to have a body for the Crothers name. Herman, who had already taken possession of the sofa, looked askance when Sebastian cheerfully plunked himself down next with a thud. Basil and Hortense pulled up conference chairs, while the sergeant expressed his preference for standing for a quick getaway.

"Frankly," Sebastian Crothers began boldly, turning his hooked nose upward and bridging his hands gothically, "I can't imagine what brings us," he looked around empathetically, "together or what possible mutual interests we have. I might say that—except for the police officer—I know the rest of you only by sight, and infrequent sight at that."

Basil's ear was catching familiar cadence and siphoning it to his brainpan. Somewhere beneath the scattered white hairs, synapses were bridged and Basil recognized the lanky fellow as Ceese's sophomoric philosophy instructor in the stacks. The text and context man. Well, well, he thought, the multicolored coat of Sebastian Crothers.

Sebastian, maintaining a priggish gaze, focused it on Herman less than two feet from him on the tufted leather sofa.

Herman's face melted into something akin to a kicked dalmation's. Hurt, however, quickly shifted to indignation with Sebastian's persistent withering glances.

"Dammit, Sebastian, you've been taking the books I put on the shelves." Herman slapped the expensive brown leather cushion.

"Come, come, Hermie. There's no need to cry our wares in the marketplace." Sebastian looked at the strangers who were hoping for a show.

Herman allowed self-righteousness to raise imperceptiveness to new heights. He ran on with his peeve. "You said you only took a couple but I know that you took whole batches—most of the stuff I bought and paid for myself and even some I bound and lettered— you know how much that cost? You said you weren't taking any more. You promised." Herman was whining.

While the Killingsleys were able to grab hold of the thread of the argument, both being intimately aware of the presence, and one the absence, of Tottel and his ilk, the sergeant was at a complete loss.

"Look, folks," he began, no longer concerned to conduct the slim business on which he came, "I don't know what you're all doing here, but my job's following through on homicide and not on missing books—whoever took them" (the sergeant glared at Sebastian) "or for whatever reason" (he turned an indifferent gaze on Herman).

"But, Sergeant," Hortense insisted in her most assertive manner, "I was trying to establish a connection. I haven't made it through to the Tottels yet, but quite evidently there's something to be made of Mr. Moraise's death and the rare books." Hortense riveted her eyes on the unwilling officer in an effort to bore through his defenses.

"Mrs. Killingsley, I'm here," he spoke slowly as if to a child, "to see Dr. Tewksbury on matters involving homicide."

Sara, seeing that the sergeant's feathers needed stroking, said, "Sergeant Kinney, if you'd bear with us for a bit, there might be something to what Dr. Killingsley said."

"No mights about it," Hortense bullied ahead, readjusting the hammerhold on her purse. "You see, Sergeant," she softened her tone, "Mr. Moraise was most certainly filching from the Smedley's rare book collections—"

Sebastian's face lit up with a smirk that proclaimed a smarmy "you don't say?"

"Mostly medieval," Basil added for accuracy.

"And," Hortense continued, trying to stay on target, "he was selling them at auction and upping the bids himself. After all, he had little to lose beyond the commission even if he found himself the high bidder. Though, come to think of it, it would take some convoluted explanation to Sotheby's as to why one would place an item on auction and then purchase it oneself, don't you think, Basil?"

"Yes, dear, but let's not lose the thread..."

"I'm only trying to fill the sergeant in on auction procedure. Well, Mr. Moraise sold several medieval works—some genuine incunabula—'' she added, noting if the officer comprehended the significance, ''and,'' she looked into the distance, ''some *not* genuine.''

''Which is where Mr. Crothers, is it? enters the picture,'' Basil added to accelerate the interest of the two on the sofa.

Sebastian Crothers's faint bemusement at Mr. Moraise's bibliographic sales erupted to alarm. Instantly, however, he regained control to look disdainfully at Basil and his tasteless suggestion.

Hortense's strategy was to let Sebastian stumble over the topic for a moment. ''In any event, Mr. Moraise was apparently using the acquired funds to purchase items for the Smedley Americana holdings—Melville, Hawthorne, Whitman, and, oh yes, was it Poe, dear? That silly *Thrice Told Tale*?''

Basil recognized his wife's putative mental contortions for what they were: a ruse to encourage the unraveling of the guilty.

''Hmm, yes,'' he responded absently. ''Though not as silly as you might think. I'd quite forgotten about it when I was on line with Dialog Library Retrieval, checking out the known Higdens, you know.''

''Uhem,'' Sergeant Kinney inserted, ''I don't mean to keep you folks from whatever tickles your professional fancies, but if you don't mind—''

''A moment! A moment, Sergeant,'' Hortense hooted in something akin to eldritch yells. She gestured for stillness to allow for coalescence of the scattered bits, but not too boldly lest she threaten the security of the Crothers fellow.

"You see, Sergeant, as it turns out, *some* of the volumes Mr. Moraise was putting up for auction," (Hortense was pressing deduction: if there was one—the Tyrwhitt Chaucer—there probably were others that Sebastian Crothers had a hand in), "well, they were not genuine, though at the time he had no idea, and no intention, I'm sure, of fraud."

"Yes, ma'am. If this library wants to make an official complaint about the books—"

"No, no, Sergeant. Please bear with me."

The sergeant sighed and decided to let the morning slip away in what might best be labeled inconsequential sociological observation. Hortense, satisfied that her audience was with her to whatever degree they dared, noting that Herman alone was self-absorbed in heavy pouting, continued. "Perhaps a specific example would help. Now let's see," she contemplated, as if selecting a choice case, "I'll spare us the Higden business and move right to the point." Sergeant Kinney sighed, smiled, and tipped back on his heels. "The Smedley copy of Thomas Tyrwhitt's edition of Chaucer."

Sara and Basil, attuned to Hortense's general direction, were carefully watching Sebastian Crothers while pretending not to. The title had its effect: not quite in league with Claudius's reaction to Hamlet's staging the play-within-the-play, but nonetheless Sebastian's facial muscles did tighten perceptibly.

As if on cue, Hortense went on. "You see, when Basil and Dr. Prout from rare books went to Sotheby's to check on the Higden that wasn't genuine, well, they were incidentally informed that Mr. Moraise had

tried to pass off a Tyrwhitt as genuine first edition—
not once, but *twice*, mind you! And they were not!''

For a moment Sara feared Sergeant Kinney was
going to toss in his sponge. Hortense, ever sensitive to
wavering vibrations, saw them flagging and whipped
out her scholastic skills that she exercised on the dull-
est of students in the driest spells of linguistic techni-
calities—even with recitation of exceptions to the rule
on diphthongization by initial palatals. Changing her
posture and pace, pitch and gesture, she carried on.
''What then, you may well wonder, were they? Fakes,
yes, to be sure. Where from, you may well wonder?
Ah! Well, Basil and Dr. Prout, having received minimal satisfaction on the Higden business, which, I need
not add, I am for the moment letting pass, they returned to the Smedley to check on the Tyrwhitt which
(mirabile dictu!) turned out to be: A) singular—that
is, one copy and not two as the gentleman at Sotheby's stated, and B) genuine. The shelf card—you do
know about shelf cards, Sergeant?''

The direct question jarred the officer from his passive reverie and he jerked back to a questionable reality. It was hard for Hortense to tell whether the
sergeant really knew about shelf cards, but in the interests of progress she was willing to let that lie in the
neither-here-nor-there category.

''Well, the shelf card indicated that the Tyrwhitt
was purchased from—Basil, who was it?—yes, Acme
Brothers in nineteen eighty-four.''

Mention of the used bookstore also had its effect on
Sebastian's already taut face.

''So off we went. My curiosity was aroused, I must
admit,'' Hortense good-humoredly rushed on, know-

ing she was getting to the good part, "and one of the Acme Brothers (personally, I doubt that the business could support more than one brother), found the records, which revealed that he—Honest Abe Acme (imagine!)—did indeed sell the Tyrwhitt to one Giles Moraise in nineteen eighty-four and that he—Honest Abe—had purchased it from one Sebastian Crothers!" Hortense fell silent and folded her arms around her purse with great satisfaction.

The sergeant looked dull. He was craving his coffee break.

Sebastian looked down at his white hands. There was a quirky movement of his brow. "There's no law against selling books!" he said in a manner echoing Herman's "There's no law against donating books."

Basil gave Hortense a nod both for a job well done and to indicate that he'd be willing to take over for the next round.

"No, no, my good man, no law at all, except when the item in question does not rightfully belong to the seller." Basil raised his white bushy brows toward Sebastian in the same way he queried recalcitrant students. While Sebastian frantically suppressed panic, the illegitimate activity Basil hinted at triggered Herman Lobel from his funk.

"God, Sebastian, you mean you were stealing real stuff? It wasn't enough kicks to take my Tottels? No, I suppose you couldn't get much for them and real work just isn't your thing. Yeah, you're a *philosopher*."

Sara was amazed at the prolixity of a fellow who had previously restricted his conversation to single syllables. Sebastian, too, was surprised at the quantity of utterance, though the greater part of his reaction stemmed from the sort of utterance. Herman's dike had evidently been unplugged, and Sebastian was ready to rush in with a finger of appeasement.

"Oh, come on, Hermie. You know I only took a few of your precious old poetry books and those merely to catch your attention."

"Oh, yeah?" Hermie responded with hurt and anger. "Then how come *she*," he tilted his head in Sara's direction, "said that all the ones I put in reference are gone? Huh, tell me that!"

Sebastian tried to look puzzled, and failing, aimed at being miffed. Meanwhile, Hortense and Basil, who had been hot in pursuit of Sebastian as rare (and not so rare) book dealer (or thief), were drinking in the Tottel business. Hortense was marveling at the sudden tidiness of the Smedley book scene and was about to comment on such, but Herman and Sebastian were not finished. Or at least Herman was not finished.

"They were mine, you know, even if I stored them on library shelves."

"Hermie, come on, there's no need to get upset over a few stupid poetry books."

"That's just it, Sebastian. You think they're stupid while...while your stuff is so grand." Hermie was not losing the opportunity to sustain his petulant character. "And you know something, Sebastian? I'm tired of you treating me like a—like a *wife*!" (At that Hortense jerked up in her chair.) "And just remember," Herman went on, oblivious of his public, "it's thanks to me that you have it so good. It's *my* job that pays the rent and its *my* job that got us furniture. You forget that if I wasn't auditor, we couldn't get—"

"Hermie, shut up." Sebastian knew things were beyond the point of pacification, and rushed to advertise the activity of least consequence. "Yes, I took that repulsive collection of Tottels, and even a couple of *Palladis Tamias*," Sebastian sneered the titles, "but I did so to save your skin."

Herman looked at his former friend with a gaze of inspired vacancy. "Huh?"

"Yes. Since you insisted on being so stupid and stuffing the shelves, I knew it was only a matter of time till you got caught. And as it turns out, I was right. Isn't that so, Dr. Tewksbury?"

Sara recognized that Sebastian was tossing the ball of argument onto another court. However, she'd play his game and leave the Killingsleys to cover their grounds of interest.

"Hmm," Sara begrudgingly assented, "Legally speaking," her eye caught the sergeant's just to see if he was still with them, "there's no law against donations—that was the term you used, wasn't it, Herman? However, morally speaking, and I might add professionally speaking, such activities leave much to be desired."

"I should think the additions well more than an insupportable irritation," Hortense chimed in. "Can you envisage a stream of Tottels populating the shelves? Why, the Smedley would either become the laughingstock of research libraries or garner a reputation for oddity worthy of *Ripley's Believe It or Not*."

"Exactly my sentiments, dear." Basil nodded. The two sat companionably for several moments when it occurred to Hortense that the comings and goings of the Tottels were the least of the problems facing the Smedley.

"Of course there're the Higdens, Tyrwhitts, and who else, dear? Oh yes, a Hilton *Scala*? And yes, Cyril did go on so about the Caxton *Eneydos*."

Hortense's list did nothing to raise Sergeant Kinney's sense of the general paucity of vice around the Smedley and he was about to state such when Sebastian Crothers let loose. "Now just a minute. One stinking minute. What's with this Hilton and Caxton garbage?" His voice was at a pitch bound to catch Ms. Gluck's ear, even through walls and doors.

"You left the Tyrwhitts off your list, Mr. Crothers."

Sebastian looked exasperated. He realized that they had the goods on him there and it would be only a matter of questioning the Acme brother more scrupulously to reveal the extent of his activity in the used-book mart.

"Yeah, Sebastian, you left the Tyrwhitts off your list," Herman taunted, though he didn't know a thing about the Tyrwhitts.

"You know, of course, that the genuine Tyrwhitt belongs not to the Smedley, but to the New York Public, from which it was stolen three years ago?" Hortense was employing her general informational tone hinting at layers of knowledge beneath the surface.

Sebastian's upper lip broke out in beads of perspiration. He was casting about as to how much or how little he need tell, or maybe that he should just let it all hang out. Things had gone farther than he imagined and he wasn't handling the fear of being caught as well as he thought. The titillation, the delightful mental frisson had been replaced by dread and insomnia. And now even his relationship with Hermie, the one promising factor in his thin existence, was dissolving before his eyes. Boy, was he a sorry mess. On the other hand, he could just make a break for it and head for L.A. With eleven dollars and change in his pocket.

"The odd thing is," Hortense continued slowly, dropping one crumb at a time, "that the New York Public didn't even know it was stolen until Dr. Prout pressed the evidence on them." She looked around and noted a wistful look of pleasure cross Sebastian's face. "Mmm. They thought they had their Tyrwhitt, but closer inspection showed it to be a later and lesser edition."

Basil was nodding in sorry recognition of being witness to the fact that a library that prides itself on its collection of forgeries should itself fall victim. The irony was both fascinating and tragic.

Sergeant Kinney was thinking he would treat himself, when this nonsense was all over, to a large sticky bun with his coffee.

"There isn't, alas, all that much interest in peripheral medievaliana these days, and not much more in the core, either." Hortense seemed to drift in her own wistful sphere. She was, however, performing, putting on her absentminded professor act to lower the guard of her prey. Of course, she, like Basil, often began in pretense and ended in earnest. She looked about as if enlightenment might be lurking in the wall paneling.

"It is for that reason, perhaps, that the New York Public wasn't aware of the dupe. Their computer files showed three Tyrwhitts, one vintage, and on the shelf was one vintage Tyrwhitt. See, dear,'' Hortense directed her remark to Basil with whom she obviously had a long-standing debate on the issue, ''computers—not yet in any event—can't tell *all*. However, it was instrumental in being able to list by day, date, and time all those who had requested that Tyrwhitt.'' Hortense paused significantly and turned her smile to Sebastian. ''I find it difficult to believe that a purported genuine Tyrwhitt would generate so little interest, but facts are facts! Indeed, Mr. Crothers, would you believe that *you* were the last person to request the Tyrwhitt, and that was over three years ago?''

''May nineteenth, nineteen eighty-four,'' Basil added for precision. ''A Saturday.''

The Killingsleys' manner had served to irritate Sebastian sufficiently that he shirked off fear and pie-eyed thoughts of flight. He chose instead to show his stuff. After all, except for a fluke—Moraise trying to auction it just after he played his little switchies—he'd have succeeded.

''Well, I ought to be congratulated, oughtn't I? I mean three years and how many supposedly knowledgeable people—and no one knew!'' Sebastian laughed inanely. ''The New York Public, one of the luminaries of the bibliographic world!'' He smirked in recollection of his challenge to the leonine New York Public which, no less than the tiny Smedley, failed in this regard. ''The Smedley, a small but ostensibly distinguished research institution! Of course, one wouldn't expect much from the likes of Abe Acme, as you have already figured out.''

"Then you did steal it?" Sara asked, just to make sure they were all on the same track.

"Let's say that I was testing the system, shall we? They say one can't walk off with a call slip from the New York Public without being detected. Actually, I had really hoped to get away with the Tyrwhitt edition of Rowley. It seemed like such a delightful cross-cultural joke, you know? That Tyrwhitt would unveil poor Chatterton's best poetic effort in trumping up Rowley and then his very exposure be the object of theft! Ah, well," Sebastian sighed affectedly, "I couldn't obtain a cheap replacement, so that was that. Instead, I persuaded my wagering friends that obtaining a Tyrwhitt Chaucer, genuine first edition, of course, would be just as good, or better, since Tyrwhitt's name was made on Chaucer—wouldn't you say, Professor?" He raised his eyebrows in query to Hortense who was too appalled to respond.

"In any event, the success of borrowing from a noncirculating library, by mere cheap substitution, mind you, buoyed my fertile brain. If one can substitute so easily and walk off with a rarity, one could up the ante."

"Excuse me, Mr. Crothers," Sergeant Kinney was back in touch with the discussion, "but how'd you get the book out the doors? Don't they have guards checking and the standard electronic apparatus?"

Sara sighed at the sergeant's naïveté.

"I'm sorry to say, Sergeant Kinney, that guards are more psychological than practical deterrents to theft. They remind the tempted, but do not inhibit the professional. And the sensors, well, they can be gotten around: books in boots or in pockets beyond the range of the detectors. Worst of all, most libraries have only the most rudimentary electronic system. I'm afraid that what the public considers standard is expensive to install and maintain, and our budgets are tight. If there's any loose change, it always goes to a current buy on some book, and security gets scuttled."

Sebastian smiled in a "precisely so" fashion.

"And you did something similar with the Higden, his *Polychronicon*, the Wynken de Worde edition of fourteen ninety-five?" Basil stabbed, figuring nothing ventured, nothing gained.

"Ah, you found that, did you? That actually was much more difficult and the margin of profit was, well, nearly nil."

Herman Lobel was looking at his former bosom buddy with new eyes. How much, he wondered, of their relationship was nearly nil?

Sebastian, noting Herman's eyes screw up in disbelief, was too carried away by his Higden caper to let it pass unsung. He explained how he obtained a facsimile, doctored it up a bit with tea soakings and the like, but then, since it looked so good, he couldn't resist testing the experts.

"You know that urge?" He looked around and no one seemed to. "Well, how many in the world would look to the *Polychronicon* for its snippets of arcane musical notation? How many eyes would read the bars?" Sebastian's voice was rising in pitch, pleading sanity in a world of lunatics who paid heed to such absurdities.

Basil quietly agreed that there were precious few Higden readers and fewer still of his musical notations from Guillaume de Machaut.

"So let me see if I have this correct, Mr. Crothers. You appropriated the Smedley Higden," Hortense hoped to disarm with feigned appreciation, "and replaced it with a doctored one. You're probably right in assuming that no one would have known. After all, when Mr. Moraise put it up for auction, he took it as genuine. But you hadn't factored in Basil. Few do. He has a flypaper brain to which everything adheres." Hortense caught herself from serious digression. "Well, now. Evidently Mr. Moraise didn't catch the switch, and neither did the people at Sotheby's. Certainly he took grave liberties selling off medievaliana, but his fraudulent intent has yet to be established."

"Come, come, now, Professor. Your wayward director—"

"Not *mine*, I assure you!"

"Moraise was up to his ears. Haven't you wondered why the Smedley director was dealing with a fence? Good ole Honest Abe Acme!"

"I *told* you, dear," Hortense said smugly now that her instincts had been corroborated.

Sebastian ignored the woman. "He was purchasing whatever he could cheaply, to fill the shelves with volumes that looked legitimate, but that (shall we say?) had a checkered past. He upped the price for library records and used the difference to buy American stuff. He even asked me to 'appropriate,' as you said, some titles. I liked to think of them as special orders. The partnership got a bit tense about six months ago when the rare books curator balked—"

"So that's why the old goat got canned!" Sara blurted.

"Ah, you are perceptive, Dr. Tewksbury. A bit slow, perhaps, but perceptive. So Moraise hires Caspar Milquetoast or whoever—"

"Are you referring to Cyril Prout? Dr. Prout happens to be . . ." Basil insisted in high dudgeon.

"Who's so busy fondling each book that he'll be a hundred and five before he gets half through. But that is not the issue. The point is, as the more astute of you have already surmised, Moraise and I figured we could each do better without the middleman and with considerably less risk." Sebastian was again filled with the cleverness of it all.

"How long did it take you, Mr. Crothers," Hortense asked in mock respect, "to realize that your little business could be even more lucrative and assuredly less risky to yourself, if you appropriated" (Sergeant Kinney winced at the deliberate and repeated misuse of the term) "not the rare editions Mr. Moraise hoped for, but editions of considerably less worth?"

Sebastian's hackles rose for a moment, but he chose to smile, bow, and give a small round of applause to Hortense's deductive skills.

"Bravo, Professor, though if you knew Moraise's passion for the American material—his 'Americana,' he was fond of calling it—you'd know that he'd have only a casual eye for other purchases. He was, you know, out to add bulk to the shelves." He glanced toward Herman with disdain. "And of course, his very presence at Acme's. . . . So, he was perfectly content to settle for third- and fourth-rate material—at not quite corresponding prices."

"For how long?" Sara asked with Killingsley perception but not patience.

"Hmm? Pardon?" Sebastian looked all innocent.

"How long did you think you could fool Giles Moraise?" It was the first time Sara had felt the slightest sense of defense for her former boss.

"Come now, Dr. Tewksbury, one plays these things by ear." Something in Sebastian's bravado was not quite authentic.

"Tell me, Dr. Tewksbury," Basil queried from nowhere, "did Mr. Moraise have the authority to fire the auditor, Leon Boehm?"

Sara looked askance, but was beginning to learn that the Killingsleys' non sequiturs fit a larger pattern. Eventually they would lead somewhere.

"No, the internal auditor is the only person who cannot be fired except by majority vote of the board. Otherwise, well, if the director were pinching... But the rest of us—legally speaking—could be zapped solely by the director's word, though in practice he would have to justify his action to the board."

"I thought so. Thank you." Basil fell back into his self-absorption, leaving an interrogative vacuum that was interrupted by a tentative knock on the door.

"Yes?"

The door opened and Ms. Gluck poked her narrow face in. "Oh, Dr. Tewksbury, I'm sorry to disturb you but..."

"Yes, Ms. Gluck? Out with it."

"This, um, gentleman here, Mr. Blinn?, insists on seeing you. He's been making a great deal of noise in the lobby and wouldn't accept the fact that you're in conference. I did tell him that this is a library and in here we keep our voices down, but—"

"Thank you, Ms. Gluck." Sara looked around at the motley group already inhabiting the office. "Sure, why not have Mr. Blinn join us?"

Cecil Blinn entered, gave a clown-face smile to Edwina Gluck, who retreated in priggish posture. Ceese howdied everyone and reintroduced himself to the sergeant. When he turned to Sebastian Crothers, he nodded without a smile, much less an invitation to friendship.

Short of disinterring the bodies of Leon Boehm and Giles Moraise, the principal actors in the Smedley drama were present. Sara hesitated asking what urgency brought Ceese in, fearing it might be something as crucial as a dinner date. Instead, she tried to weave Ceese into the cloth that was about.

"You two know each other?" she asked Ceese with regard to Sebastian, knowing full well of their limited acquaintance.

"You could say that," Ceese said with a hint of uncharacteristic disdain, "though the knowing is some lopsided." He let the comment hang cryptically in the air.

Sebastian's eyebrows rose and his mouth turned down in a "you-don't-say" smirk.

"You folks having a meeting of the minds? Clearing up the mess around this place?" Ceese was back in his Texas-friendly mode.

"You could say that," Basil responded, happily echoing Ceese's cadence.

"Got to the part about who done in who?"
"Not yet."
"Good."

FOURTEEN

CECIL BLINN HAD A BUSY weekend finding out the good part. He felt the urge to make sense of the oddities shooting up like oil from uncapped wells. Leaving aside two deaths and screwed-up book tallies, there was that strange fellow in the baggy trousers who talked nonsensically about editions and perspectives, and who walked off with a Tottel. When the Killingsleys connected the crammed-pocketed, baggy-trousered fellow to the Tyrwhitt business, well, it seemed to Ceese that the rabbit was begging to be chased to its hole.

"Come Saturday morning," he explained to the assembled group as Sebastian yawned, "I says to myself, why not see what's what?" Everyone turned to Ceese except Sebastian Crothers who was pretend dozing and Herman Lobel who was moving his lips obscenely.

"Ya see, the night before—that'ud be Friday night—after me and Mizz Tewksbury had ourselves a soo-per supper," Ceese goggled in Sara's direction, "I set myself to readin' more of that Holinshed book the professor here gave me. You folks know Holinshed's *Chronicles*?"

Sergeant Kinney looked like he had just had enough and wasn't about to expend his remnant of sanity on a Texan's recitation of pseudo-history.

"Basil could tell us of the *Chronicles'* embrangled publication record," Hortense invited. "Apparently Holinshed was so tactless in treating virtually contemporaneous events that the second edition—posthumous—"

"Has any of this anything to do with anything?" the officer pleaded.

Hortense looked at him as if he were mad to spurn a free education, while Ceese grabbed back the topic he had so recently learned of. "Yessirree, 'cause without old Holinshed around the second edition got ex-purr-gated. Ya know, now there ain't a single genuine first edition around—not even for a million bucks!"

"Let's not overlook the British Museum," Basil added with expansive interest.

The sergeant's indifference to bibliographic history was becoming palpable. Before he could yet again moan his query for relevance, Ceese jumped in, his beady eyes bulging in animation. "Righto! That's what got me thinkin'. Ya see, Sarge, I'm comin' to my point. The professor here told me all about Holinshed—his *Chronicles*, that is, and about there bein' just one original copy in the whole world that has the whole story as the fella set it down. Now the funny thing is that this one original ain't even a genuine first edition, but it's got the cut-out pages—"

"Canceled pages," Basil noted with quiet authority.

"That's right—the canceled pages. They were put into a second edition so's that's how we know about them in the first place. A com-posite edition." Ceese looked pleased at his ability to plummet the arcane world of bibliography, especially as he had spent less than three weeks in it.

"The point?" Sergeant Kinney pleaded.

"Oh, righto. My point is..." Ceese looked around trying to locate his point. "Oh, yessirree. Well, there I was readin' the grizzly stories in Holinshed and I was just finishin' the one about this here king killin' off his little nephews and buryin' 'em—"

"Richard. Richard the Third."

"The point?" the sergeant persisted, oblivious of the dramatic proprieties the two men were cultivating.

"I'm gettin' there, Sarge. Well, just at the end of the story, the book tells that it's includin' the canceled pages so's a person can know what's what. The pages tell about the hired murderers—one of 'em was still alive—"

"John Dighton," Basil offered. "The other was Miles Forrest."

"Yup, that's them. Well, I got to thinkin'..." the sergeant looked as if something faintly ridiculous had crossed his mind, "that maybe that's a way some books around here look genuine and turn out to be fake."

Basil and Hortense acknowledged pellucid logic lurking in Ceese's train of thought. Sara, too, gave credit to Ceese's associational skills, which seemed to evidence something more than a smattering of intelligence.

"Bein' as I'm not up on all the angles in books, I figured to rope in Doc Prout so's we could mosey off to the folks at Sotheby's and ask a few more questions. Old Cyr thought it'd be a good idea to bring along the Tyrwhitt to make sure *it* was gen-yu-ine.''

Basil nodded appreciatively. "And you undoubtedly indicated the despicable inkblot primitively concealing the New York Public's imprint?'' he asked, jutting his brows in Sebastian's direction.

"We sure as hell did. We talked with the fella who knows all about Tyrwhitt—the expert fella who told Mr. Moraise that his were fakes. So this fella, Archie Smythe, he's real accommodatin' and gets out the records and—just a minute—'' Ceese fished his pockets to retrieve a slip of paper. He was cottoning to his investigatory role. "Ah, here it is, yessirree. Mr. Moraise came in on June twenty-first with a book that turned out to have the front page—that'ud be the title page—of a first edition, but the rest of that there book was from eighteen fifty.'' Ceese looked up from his notepaper with satisfaction. "It was just like I thought—not a gen-yu-ine first edition. It was one of them com-posite editions.'' Ceese looked around, tickled by his insights. Basil shared the appreciation for the truth, while Sebastian sighed in a fresh effort at metaphysical speculation of his fingernails.

"Well this here Mr. Smythe tells us Mr. Moraise comes in again with another Tyrwhitt on,'' Ceese checked his notes, "June the twenty-fourth in the afternoon. Now get this: Mr. Smythe tells him *it's* fake and so Mr. Moraise just about blows up. Mr. Smythe says he left the place fit to kill.'' Ceese paused for murmurs and gasps. None was forthcoming. Only Sebastian's shut eyelids twitched a little; and others (minus muttering Herman) were expecting Ceese to make his point.

"You folks recall June the twenty-fourth?"

Hortense remembered it as her half birthday. Basil rummaged more abstractly: no, it certainly wasn't Pearl Harbor, the Bastille, VJ Day, or another summer landmark. He juggled feverishly with historic possibilities, and looking at Sara with his inner vision, asked dubiously, "The Battle of Tewkesbury? No, no, that's in May and so few celebrate what was, after all, a minor skirmish over four hundred years ago—well, minor except to Margaret and Prince Edward. Ah well, all right, Ceese," Basil checked to see if there were any other takers, "tell us—June twenty-fourth—we are speaking of this year?"

"Yessiree. A Monday."

"Giles was killed," Sara said quietly, recalling more the day than date.

"Ah, good, good, Ceese," Basil confirmed, nodding his head affably as pieces fell into place.

"This is all very boring, if you don't mind my saying so," Sebastian Crothers said, stifling a pretend yawn. "I can't fathom the satisfaction the lot of you feel at having established the day and date of your director's demise, as this information is readily available. Perhaps even from Sergeant Kinney?"

The sergeant stood immobile, unwilling to side with a fellow about whom there were collecting too many confused and refractory particulars.

"And, though you may find it hard to believe, I do have better things to do than commemorate occasions with which I have not even the remotest concern." Sebastian slid forward and was about to rise from the sofa when Sergeant Kinney suggested he stick around for a while. The officer's voice did not leave much room for choice.

"Thanks, Sarge," Ceese said. "It's just sort of convenient to have everybody in one spot."

Herman Lobel looked around at everybody and wondered what factors made it convenient to have them in one spot. He entropically considered his own concerns: the Tottels? Naw, there was no crime in donating. The furniture he—really Sebastian—got for the apartment? What did the lot of them have to do with that, except maybe Tewksbury? And, besides, like Sebastian said, he didn't order any stuff for the office, so he was getting only what was due to him. Herman mentally grazed for other connections, but the strain obscured even the reason that brought him to this gathering in the first place.

Hortense, too, mulled the shreds and shards, though in her case, her rife brain yielded fact. "That was the day you, Basil, and Cyril were at the auction, and you repurchased—no, purchased—the doctored Higden." She crinkled her brow. "And Mr. Moraise was there upping the bids. Why, he must have had the Tyrwhitt appraised..." She let the rest of the sequence drift.

Sebastian, feeling the weight of the air heavy with insinuation, blurted his alibi. "Well, if we're to account for our whereabouts for the afternoon, I for one was helping my friend here," he turned to Herman, darting a saccharin smile, "perhaps my *former* friend here. He was contemplating his prospects in light of his new position as auditor. Remember, Hermie, we were in your apartment sipping—Ricard, was it? and reading—oh, ha, yes! How delicious, how simply fabulous! We were reading Tottel!''

Herman strained stuporously to verify Sebastian's June twenty-fourth whereabouts. The scene sounded familiar; he remembered getting on Sebastian for taking the Tottels and he promised not to take more. The events stumbled around in his head. Suddenly a synapse was bridged. The shit.

He jutted out a weak chin upholding a glowering sneer. ''That wasn't Monday afternoon: it was Monday *evening* and I distinctly remember that we decided to—'' Hermie stopped short for reasons of discretion. ''Never mind, but that was Monday *evening*!''

Sebastian looked about innocently as if afternoon and evening were all one. His inner recesses, however, calculated how to pull trumps on Herman whom he had apparently misjudged, and misjudged badly. Nothing worse than a poor sniveling sport. And Herman really did need the guidance of someone brighter. Ah, well, Sebastian thought, if I have to do without the accouterments I've helped him acquire, so will he.

''Wasn't it the evening we were arranging furniture in your ratty apartment? Yes, the stuff you ordered from National Office Suppliers since you, Herman, were, and I do mean *were*, auditor and thought you could appropriate a few freebies.'' Sebastian cackled, waiting for his red herring to be chased.

Sara recognized National as the Smedley supplier, and recalled seeing an invoice from them for a variety of unorthodox items. However, as she assumed there was a mistake, she had put the bill aside for quieter times.

Herman Lobel, meanwhile, fully aware of his former friend's attempt to cast suspicion his way, ran after the herring. "Why, you—you miserable leech. You—you cock—"

"Ahem," Sara interposed to halt whatever nasty epithets Herman's limited imagination was striving for.

"All right, Sebastian, if that's the way you want it! Yeah, so I got stuff from National Office Suppliers, but it was *your* idea and you even picked the stuff out!"

Sebastian Crothers sat paring his fingernails with pacific disdain. "I suppose, Hermie, you're going to tell everyone that garnering supplies like sofa beds and wall hangings isn't stealing," he said without shifting attention from his hands. "To say nothing of the reams of paper toweling and toilet tissue you stashed away."

"That's a matter the Smedley board will have to decide." Basil Killingsley spoke with authority, eager to put the herring chase at an end. "However, such appropriations do not preclude the issue of your whereabouts on the Monday afternoon in question, Mr. Crothers."

Sebastian interrupted his fingernail examination long enough to give Basil a suggestive glare. He exerted every effort at nonchalance. "If you insist, I was at home reading Wittgenstein. For my dissertation, you know."

Herman Lobel screwed up his eyes in an effort to assimilate his former friend's alibi. His facial creases eased as a small epiphany crept over his mottled, lumpy visage.

"You dirty liar! I remember now. I tried calling you and you weren't home. There was nothing doing around here," Sara darted a quizzical look at Herman for his assessment of indolence at the Smedley, "and—oh, never mind. I got busy in the reference room and around three or so I looked out the window and *there you were*!"

Basil glanced at Hortense. Ceese sighed and folded his arms. He looked up and reluctantly confirmed Herman's accusation.

"Old Cribbs—that guy at the entrance? He said the same. He didn't know the name, but he sure's heck knew the baggy trousers when they ran past his desk just about three. He remembers in particular," Ceese said thoughtfully in Sebastian's direction, "'cause you usually just march on through the sensors real normal like even when your pockets are all stuffed. But this time Old Cribbs recollects that you just about flew down the stairs and out the door in a whizz. He says you barely had time to open the door. He remembers it bein' around three 'cause that's just about when he takes his break."

"And that was just about the time you," Hortense nodded at Sebastian, "nearly bolted me over in the lobby. I simply assumed you were a scholar pursuing some point a bit overzealously." She stared at him questioningly, and continued. "When we were introduced a while ago, I remembered your name from Mr. Acme. But your appearance struck a chord I couldn't place. Now, you see, I've placed it." She sighed with satisfaction as if the *raison d'être* of the group had at last been fulfilled.

Basil acknowledged his wife's recollection as yet another ounce of mortar cementing the case.

Sebastian's attempt at disembodied consciousness was betrayed by his adrenal glands operating at full tilt. His face was mottled and glistening with beads of sweat. No consolation of philosophy seemed possible.

"And what's all this supposed to mean? That I did in old Moraise? And over a lousy book? Come on now!" He gave a laugh that was as false as his bravado.

"Was it just a lousy book? Come, come, Mr. Crothers." Hortense spoke with a sense of confidence suggesting everyone knew the truth and to attempt further concealment was not merely foolish, but embarrassingly gauche.

"You had been deceiving Mr. Moraise—or shall we say the Smedley?—for some time. According to Dr. Prout, the rare books shelves were not only quantitatively thinning, despite, I might add, Mr. Lobel's ludicrous contributions, but the quality was deteriorating perceptibly. This, Cyril told us," Hortense looked to Basil for support she really didn't need, "had been happening for as long as he's been here—over six months now. He hesitated bringing the problem to Mr. Moraise without substantial and irrefutable proof, especially in light of Mr. Moraise's low threshold for such matters. No doubt Cyril had an inkling of what had happened to his predecessor." Hortense raised her eyebrows knowingly. "Well, after just one too many clear instances of devastation, his professional concern outweighed personal considerations and he summoned courage to present the matter to Mr. Moraise." Hortense paused to allow Cyril's bravery its due recognition. "As he anticipated, Mr. Moraise was not receptive, and as a matter of fact, told him to mind his own business!" Hortense grimaced at the small irony which, as she looked around, she saw others had not seen. "You see, Dr. Prout *was* minding his own business!"

Basil nodded sympathetically to his marveling wife and took up the pursuit. "When Cyril did not receive satisfaction, he escalated his endeavors in a twofold manner—one not entirely legitimate, but sustained by higher scruples—demonstrating his overriding concern for the irreplaceable, the nearly priceless treasures..."

Basil drifted into charitable reverie just as Hortense returned from hers. She grabbed the argumentative thread of her choice. "It doesn't matter, dear. Sara and the board know about Cyril's safeguarding volumes in his apartment. He was clearly *safeguarding* and not *appropriating*!" she said with pointed significance toward Sebastian.

"Yes, that's true," Basil confirmed, still prepared to publicly defend Cyril's questionable security measures. "After all, if one's own director isn't alarmed—nay, is *himself* disgracefully engaged in deception—well, then, one is indeed in an ethical bog."

Sara saw that the discussion had incrementally shifted to peripheral grounds. She picked it up and moved it to its original site. "Dr. Prout also went to the board of directors and told them what he knew and what he suspected—"

"Of course," Hortense interrupted, "at the time poor Cyril had no idea that Mr. Moraise was involved."

"The board was naturally concerned and questioned Leon Boehm, the auditor. That was on the tenth."

"A Monday, wasn't it, dear?" Hortense inserted, eager to keep the facts aligned. "Mondays are not the happiest days at the Smedley, are they?"

"Monday, June tenth. They had had a meeting on Friday the seventh when Cyril presented his case."

"And Mr. Boehm supplied the board with shocking figures."

"Yes, so incongruent," Sara confirmed, "that there were rumblings of replacing Giles! When Giles got wind of things, you can imagine his reaction. He wasn't one to sit passively under siege."

Hortense's eyes lit up. "And I'll bet my bun warmer that's when he personally delivered his dreadful evaluation to Mr. Boehm. Late Monday, possibly Tuesday." She crinkled her forehead, straining for factual precision. "Basil, remember that extremely injudicious letter lying under Mr. Boehm's head? It contained scandalous accusations about his accounting abilities."

"Yes, dear."

"When we found his body on Wednesday you thought its incriminating placement obviated suspicion of Mr. Moraise—"

"But, my dear—"

"I'm more certain than ever that Mr. Moraise deliberately left that vile evaluation just so we'd reason that such motive was planted and he was being framed. He probably had words with Mr. Boehm and the situation got out of control—*his* control. He grabbed the first likely weapon—the computer cable. I mean, it isn't as if an accounting office has an abundance of lead pipes or cyanide pills.'' Hortense sat wide-eyed, taking to her fabrications.

Sergeant Kinney, who was taking in the erratic arguments and trying to sort conjecture from fact, was puzzled by one piece that fell neither here nor there. "You said that you're sure Moraise delivered the letter of evaluation to Boehm personally. How d'ya know?"

"Sergeant, office mail is dated and delivered once a day, early morning, is that not so, Dr. Tewksbury?"

Sara nodded.

"My husband and I, along with Mr. Blinn and Dr. Tewksbury, found Mr. Boehm's body on Wednesday afternoon and it was cold. Rigor mortis and all. He had to have been dead a full day or two at the least. Well, while my husband and I were guarding the body, we took the opportunity to investigate the premises. I went for the trash on the proven tenet that one learns more from a person's trash than his or her diary. Well, there was no date of receipt on the letter itself and no delivery envelope in the trash: ergo, the letter did not go through interoffice mail. It was personally delivered.'' Hortense fell silent and locked her arms about her generous breast, certain that her argument clarified matters for the densest of minds.

Sergeant Kinney looked a little screwily at her but conceded a shred of logic in the woman's reasoning. He also realized that since both Boehm and Moraise were dead, if one did do in the other, it would save state money in prosecution.

"All right, we'll consider that."

As the case was being built against Giles Moraise, it slowly came to Herman Lobel that his starring role as suspect in Leon Boehm's murder held no such stature. He did not take offense that no one save Sebastian had ever even credited him with the deed. Instead, he used his new comprehension as ammunition against his former buddy.

"So there, Sebastian. I told you I had nothing to do with Boehm's death." He turned to the others. "He was gonna be real big and supply me with an alibi since how the hell am I supposed to remember where I was every minute that week?"

Somehow Sergeant Kinney, like the greater share of the Smedley staff, had overlooked the person of Herman Lobel, never mind allotting him a principal part in the drama. Out of pure charity, the sergeant acknowledged the wimpy figure's case. "Yes, Mr. Lobel. We understand. Not many people remember their daily whereabouts. It's normal."

Hortense glared as if the officer had expanded the definition of normal beyond linguistic bounds. However, as the facts led elsewhere than to Herman Lobel, she personally closed the issue of Boehm's demise and opened that of Moraise's.

"I trust, Officer, that your definition of normalcy does not encompass bashing oneself on the back of the head?"

"No, ma'am." Sergeant Kinney was back wishing he'd gone for coffee and sticky buns.

"Then I demand that you arrest this man," she stood and pointed to Sebastian Crothers in her best Perry Mason fashion, "or else I shall be forced to make a citizen's arrest!"

Sergeant Kinney rolled his eyes upward while Herman Lobel audibly mumbled, "Yeah, arrest the fucker."

FIFTEEN

As soon as the Smedley board of directors voted Sara Tewksbury the promotion from acting to permanent director, Ceese insisted on throwing a celebration dinner at the very expensive and posh Chez Robert. Everyone connected with the recent events at the Smedley was invited—with the understandable exceptions of the deceased and the criminal. For reasons of logic and expedience, Leon Boehm's death was ruled homicide accidentally committed by Giles Moraise. Giles's death—unpremeditated murder—was still open and shut as Sebastian Crothers was placed under close observation at the State Institute for Mental Health. Herman Lobel, too, was absent from this festive occasion, having been relieved of his responsibilities as auditor. He had agreed, under threat of joining his former friend at the state's expense, to locate and remove whatever remained of his unorthodox Tottels from the Smedley shelves.

As the waiter uncorked another magnum of champagne, Ceese chuckled at the overflowing foam and Hortense raised her glass for more.

"The odd thing is…" she asserted too loudly so that the table's conversations stopped mid-phrase.

"Well, you needn't all stare as if I were a specimen," she continued, sitting straighter for her audience.

"I merely find it odd that Acme Brothers purchased the Tyrwhitt copies—both of them! We saw them in their filthy window just last week, didn't we, Basil?"

Basil looked doubtfully at his wife, inured to her selection of what was odd.

"You do all see what I mean?"

"Perhaps Acme foresees a Tyrwhitt revival?" Cyril Prout ventured, smiling benignly under the influence.

Miss Sisson, sitting next to Cyril Prout, found his remark eminently amusing and giggled foolishly. She, too, had been imbibing at an unaccustomed rate, partly in celebration that reference room tallies were back to normal, and partly because she liked the bubbles up her nose.

"Oooo," she cooed, raising her glass again.

"I betcha they got a real bargain," Ceese cheerily bolstered when no one else took up the chase.

"It certainly won't help our circulation tally," Edwina Gluck added soberly, fingering her champagne flute hoping to display her bony hands to advantage.

"You're missing the point," Hortense insisted, surprised that such density could reign amid these professed bibliophiles.

"Their sale leaves the Smedley quite bereft of Tyrwhitt. The genuine one is back at the New York Public."

Hortense's conclusion was met with virtual indifference, except from Basil who knew the mechanics of his wife's mind.

"Ah, but they were gracious enough to trade the Higden—the *Smedley* Higden, the fourteen ninety-five

Wynkyn de Worde, G. van Os initialed Higden, obtained at auction, for the much less worthy Tyrwhitt,'' he rejoiced, daring anyone to challenge the profitable nature of the swap.

"Sure nice of them folks at Sotheby's to let us keep the fake one. I been givin' it a good readin'." Ceese spoke, screwing up his large round face in an attempt to recall an episode or two for illustration.

"It's all well and good unless you try to make sense of the musical notations," Hortense added, index finger raised in warning at their host across the table.

"I dinna ken, Mizz Killingsley," Barney Dibbs, to the right of Ceese, called across the table. He had carefully considered Hortense's nomination for odd thing and he wished to offer an alternative. "I haen teuk the verra ferlie ta be the findin' o' the auld Shakespeare 'atween the covers of—whatna?—the auld Tottel!"

Edna Leddy, sitting catercorner to her fiancé, snapped out of her trance at the mention of Tottel. She had a lot to thank him for.

"Here, here," Hortense announced, reveling in Barney's superb glottal stop. "Well said, Barney. Does everyone know about that fortuitous find?"

"Dear, this isn't a seminar." Basil held his and his wife's glasses up as the waiter came by.

"Oh, but it's such poetic justice! Miss Sisson, you were there for the find . . . ?"

A second of blank silliness swept over Winifred, but she recalled herself when Edwina Gluck, opposite, nodded encouragingly while masticating a crudité.

"It was that Herman Lobel," Ms. Gluck carried on for her colleague. She was pointing her celery stick in meaningful accusation. "When he was ordered to re-move his silly additions from the shelves, well, you see it was a question of either accepting the blame for theft of the Shakespeare or disclaiming the whole nonsense." Having made the issue manifestly clear to herself, Edwina resumed examination and consump-tion of her stringy crudité.

Edna Leddy, eager to hang on to her role in the ex-citement, was pleasantly struggling toward compre-hension. She was in something of a haze what with the champagne and her recent, heady engagement. She looked to her fiancé for clarification. M. Farb was happily relaxed with one hand enclosing Edna's and the other resting on a large envelope half concealed by his linen napkin. He nodded as the waiter offered to pour more of his native elixir.

"Yessirree, that Sebastian Crothers sure's a slick fella," Ceese sighed, relaxing back in his chair. "Pre-tendin' he's takin' Tottels—and sometimes he's doin' just that and sometimes he's doin' a whole lot more. Musta gotten nervous, or maybe his pockets got full to the brim and he had to leave that one behind. Wowee, some folks sure in hell got nerve."

"I don't think I understand," Edna spoke, won-dering how she could have missed an episode in the Tottel affair.

"Well, Mrs. Leddy," Sara volunteered to summa-rize the Shakespearean caper, "Sebastian Crothers knew that the Tottels and their covers could be freely removed from the library as they lacked the metal sensors. However, as they weren't worth much, he figured to make greater profit by wrapping rare texts in the Tottel covers—"

"And that contributed to the Tottel confusion,"
Hortense burst in. "What with the oddly labeled covers on cheap Tottels, thanks to Mr. Lobel, and then
thanks to the Crothers fellow exchanging Tottel texts
for the likes of Shakespeare, well, you can see how he
hoped to smuggle rarities right from under everyone's nose. My God—not hoped—he did!"

Edna was still puzzled. "But why didn't he just tear
the covers off the valuable books?"

"He had to have a backup if he got caught. He'd
have pretended he was playing a private game with
Herman: Herman as a joke placing non-Smedley
books on shelves; Sebastian as a joke removing non-
Smedley books from shelves. And no harm done."

"No harm done? Joke?" Hortense shrieked, indicating her low tolerance for those who misuse books.
Before offering full explication of her outrage and
proof of the real harm the Tottel nonsense engendered, Hortense found herself with the olive tray in
one hand and the salmon mousse platter in the other.
There wasn't space to put either plate down. Basil
noted his wife's dilemma.

"Dear, you mustn't hog the hors d'oeuvres. Ah,
superb, these nice plump Sicilians." He plopped an
olive into his mouth and turned back to the conversation.

Cyril Prout, on Hortense's right, noticed her search
for a clear space. He made bumbling gestures to shift
cutlery and bowls, knocking over an empty glass.

"Oh, thank you. I've the identical problem at
home. Basil and I wouldn't find the phone but for its
ring. We're forever shifting piles in futile attempts to
find space, but I'm afraid we're only playing out *The*

Woman in the Dunes. You do know the film? It made
me want to vacuum my whole house. At the time, as I
recall, I couldn't locate the vacuum.''

Basil caught his wife's drift. He would have to rescue Cyril.

''Tell me, Cyril, have the rarities been cataloged yet?
I'm eager to examine our generous friend's purchases.''

Michel Farb, at the table's end, overheard Basil's
query and nodded affably to indicate recognition of
the Smedley's latest and largest philanthropist.

''Ah, it's come through then, has it?'' Basil winked
and nodded down the table. Michel Farb raised his
glass affirmatively and tapped the large envelope.

''Well, you'd best get to it,'' Hortense leaned toward Michel, blocking Basil's path to the olives, ''or
the lot of us will be besotted and beyond appreciation.'' She rolled her eyes diagonally opposite where
Ceese was roaring with laughter and slathering heaps
of pink spread on a roll. Sara Tewksbury, sitting next
at the far end, was also vivacious with gestures send-
ing her bangles and beads helter-skelter. Everyone was
well on his or her way to being sloshed, even Ms.
Gluck, who, although aware that the table was generating more than its fair share of noise, generously let
slip the opportunity to issue a sanctimonious
''shhh...''

M. Farb looked questioningly at Sara at the opposite head, and after a quick survey of the table, she
nodded. Michel put down his champagne, stood
slowly, and tapped the flute for silence.

"This evening, *mesdames et messieurs—*" he looked around to briefly acknowledge each party "—I have good fortune to bring very special news."

Edna Leddy looked down in blissful embarrassment, preparing herself to stand graciously at the announcement of their engagement.

Ceese beamed and elbowed Sara to alert her to imminent public acceptance of her new official post as director of the Smedley.

Cyril Prout straightened his bow tie in readiness for his speech on the importance of constant vigilance in rare books.

Edwina Gluck cleared her throat, ready to accept whatever credit was about to be bestowed on her.

Barney Dibbs and Winifred Sisson, sitting together, were juggling for a common conversational language. His Celtic brogue and her inebriated slurring rendered them momentary solipsists. They had missed M. Farb's call and were deeply into the refuge their lobster bisque offered.

"*Ah, oui,*" Michel continued in a thick Maurice Chevalier accent that registered in Barney and Winifred's sensitive ears. They quietly put down their spoons.

"This is, to be sure, an occasion for much celebration on many accounts." His deep-set eyes twinkled. "*Au premier,* we have a grand debt of gratitude to pay to our host and benefactor, M. Blinn." Michel opened his arm in Ceese's direction and initiated the round of applause. Ceese nodded and waved off the fuss.

"And *naturellement*, the occasion for which we present ourselves this evening is one that gives me *personellement* much pleasure. That is, to be sure, the official appointment of our new director." Michel raised his glass in toast. "Mesdames, messieurs, I present *tous les vous* with Dr. Sara Tewksbury, the choice—*sans* exception—of the Smedley board."

Ceese led off the applause with enthusiasm and his were the last claps concluding the Smedlian overture. He grinned and helped Sara to rise. She swept her unruly hair behind her ears, bangled her bracelets, and stood tall. In the ensuing hush, Ms. Gluck again cleared her throat. Sara began:

"This is too nice a time to spoil with speeches. I just want to thank the board of directors for their confidence in me and I, too, wish to acknowledge the generosity of our host, Mr. Blinn. As you all know, the Smedley has just weathered some rough times, and with the help of many of you—Mr. Blinn, Mrs. Leddy, Dr. Prout, and, of course, the Professors Killingsley—we've come through and are back on track. I hope I may lead the Smedley to greater fulfillment of its scholarly mission. Thank you all."

"Here, here." Hortense irrepressibly waved her glass. "A brilliant choice with proof right here in the pudding."

Several looked about curiously to locate the pudding.

"Why, brevity of speech furnishes substantial evidence of administrative acumen." Her eyes grazed the group for unanimity, and finding what they sought, she clinked her glass with Cyril's on her right, which set off the chain of clinking and clanking to the accompaniment of murmurs expressing nice things.

"Sit down, dear," Basil whispered to his wife, "or you'll terrify these decent people with the fear of a lecture on your latest catch in Grimm's Law."

Having herself imbibed slightly more than usual, with only olives and carrot sticks to soak up the alcohol, Hortense dropped back into her chair and emitted a tiny burp. She felt relieved. Her husband's mention of Grimm allowed her to be pleasantly reminded that indeed she had tracked down irrefutable evidence on the post-Conquest drift of particular labial stops among the native English as a result of the Anglo-Norman influence. Furthermore, she happily ruminated, her investigations coincided and converged with Basil's on the Anglo-Norman roots of (much later) English imperialistic policies.

Michel Farb retrieved the floor by again tapping his glass and raising his graceful hands. He picked up the thin, large envelope from under his bisque bowl.

"I am most certain you are eager to enjoy the excellent meal before us and I do not wish to delay that happy experience. However, there is one additional surprise. May I ask that our host, M. Cecil Blinn, arise, *s'il vous plaît*?"

Ceese looked around as if to check for another Cecil Blinn. He raised himself in some embarrassment.

"Ah, M. Blinn, we are all aware that your generosity far exceeds this evening's celebration. Your many and (shall we say?) substantial donations to the Smedley have permitted her to regain her former status as the grande dame of research libraries. Your exceptional patronage of rare books has made our collection supreme and earned for yourself our lasting gratitude. *(Je le dis: toujours.)* On this account especially, we have that which I hope is *une bonne surprise*." Michel opened the envelope and removed a bronze plaque.

"May I present this token to you, to be placed—I believe next month—on the occasion of ground-breaking," M. Farb was aware of the moment's drama, "of the Cecil Blinn Wing of Incunabula!"

Ceese's eyes popped in disbelief. He barely heard the applause or felt the pats on the back. He saw Sara nodding happily and knew Truth. She was the woman of his dreams. It was all too much. He absently shook Michel's hand and received the plaque. He waved off vague pleas for speech, too choked to speak.

Hortense Killingsley, never at a loss for words, thought she might shift attention from the astounded Texan, but when she opened her mouth, she found it filled with emotion.

Basil, on the other hand, had rapidly calculated the situation and moved to get the party back in swing. He picked up his spoon to orchestrate. "Come now, ladies and gentlemen. The bisque will freeze in our bowls if we don't go to. Plenty of opportunity for plaque examination when it's hanging."

"Dear, you make it sound like a visit to the dentist. Ah, but your point is taken. Dear friends, do as my husband says." She raised her spoon in demonstration and went to.

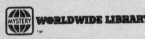

"Hornsby's work shows a skillful sleight-of-hand that borders on witchcraft."

—Hartford Courant

NOHARM

WENDY HORNSBY

A young woman's life becomes endangered when she inherits a palatial California estate. Several near-fatal accidents fuel her growing fear as she searches through generations of buried secrets and deadly deceptions to find the portrait of a family killer.

"Suspenseful tale features Gothic atmosphere
and a small-town Southern setting."
—*Booklist*

CRY AT
DUSK

MIGNON F. BALLARD

A woman comes face-to-face with her darkest nightmare when she returns to her small hometown to investigate the death of her cousin and learns the secret of not
one murder but two.

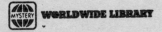

ATTRACTIVE, SPACE SAVING BOOK RACK

Display your most prized novels on this handsome and sturdy book rack. The hand-rubbed walnut finish will blend into your library decor with quiet elegance, providing a practical organizer for your favorite hard-or soft-covered books.

Only $9.95

Approximately 16" x 8" when assembled

Assembles in seconds!

To order, rush your name, address and zip code, along with a check or money order for $10.70* (9.95 plus 75¢ postage and handling) payable to *The Mystery Library Reader Service.*

Mystery Library Reader Service
Book Rack Offer
901 Fuhrmann Blvd.
P.O. Box 1396
Buffalo, NY 14269-1396

Offer not available in Canada.

BKR-ML

* New York and Iowa residents add appropriate sales tax.